Death In The High Lonesome

Mac Crow #2

![illustration]

By Clint Hollingsworth

Illustration by Clint Hollingsworth

www.clinthollingsworth.com
Printed in the United States of America
ISBN: 978-0-9975170-0-2

Cover design by Clint Hollingsworth and Jeannine Henning

Dedication

*Dedicated to my Grampa Slim
and Gramma Janie Hollingsworth,
wherever their souls may be camping.*

CHAPTER ONE

It was late.

He stood in the doorway, looking across the desks, and noted the flashing message lights on one of the phones. After walking across the room, he punched the play button to listen.

"Cousin, somethin's up. Been bein' watched, and someone broke into m' cabin. Goin' to ground for a while, so's I can see who's doing the huntin'. Meet me day after tomorrow at our old place. I'll tell you what I've found so far on them questions you had 'bout the meth. Later."

The man looked down at the recorder on the desk, glanced out the door and saw there was no one to see.

"Oh, we can't have that," he said to himself.

Message erased.

CHAPTER TWO

It's possible I may hate Robert Dade.

I thought this as my feet went toward the ceiling, while my shoulders fell toward the thin mat we'd been battling on.

I snapped my right arm out and as my upper torso hit, I slapped and yelled as loud as I could in order to harden my body for absorbing the impact. Unfortunately, this was my only free arm, and I couldn't get it back in time to block the thunderous punch coming in at my floating ribs. I tried to twist away, but the punch connected, though by no means as hard as it could have. It did make me short of breath, but I kept trying to free my arm and counter attack.

"Yamé! Stop!" yelled the referee in his baggy white pants and T-shirt. "Point to red!"

Then, (and only then), I and my opponent, fourth-degree black belt Robert Dade Sensei, stopped trying to neutralize each other. "Score, red has two, white has one! Take your positions!"

I could feel my heart pounding with adrenalin as I looked for any weakness in his stance. I was a Ni-Dan, a second-degree black belt, and I had proved earlier that I was the faster of the two of us by drawing "first blood" with my best move, a quick sidekick that tagged him directly in the chest. I thought I had him then, but I was wrong. He had merely grinned at me as I set up to see if I could hit him with it again. As I started to move forward he had simply come forward when the referee signaled start and grabbed the shoulder of my white uniform, kicking my front foot to the vicinity of Mars.

And he had just done it a second time.

This time, both my feet had gone flying, and truth be told, I was a little shaky, inside and out. I started to set in my sideways fast-kick stance, when Dade Sensei looked at my feet and raised his eyebrow at me. His message was clear.

You gonna let me do that again?

I may be slow, but I can learn. I switched my feet to a three-quarter forward stance and started moving. I tried to stay cat-like, avoiding the silly jumping around that some of the fighters here seemed to think was a good idea and when I saw Dade drop his guard a moment later, I pounced.

"Saaa!" I yelled as I snapped out my right, following with a left trying to drive my opponent back. He slapped aside the first punch then raised his right arm to block the second.

Gotcha!

I spun and kicked back with my right heel at the ribs he had just exposed, only he wasn't quite where he was supposed to be. He had shifted his body slightly so that my kick grazed his ribs and then went past him. I felt his hand grab my shoulder,....

Then I was looking up at him and the ref through a sea of stars.

I raised my hands up in defense, but the ref put his hand on my chest as I tried to get up.

"Whoa, son!" He grinned. "It's over, we're puttin' a fork in you. You're done."

****

Later, in the locker room of our dojo, Sensei Dade came up and clapped me on the shoulder. "You doing okay there, Mac?"

"Hai," I affirmed formally. "Thanks for asking, Sempai."

"Ha! No need to be so formal, unless you're piqued at me for repeatedly introducing you to the floor out there."

"You're the senior student, Sensei Dade. I guess it's not surprising that you 'schooled' me out there."

He looked down. "Well, schooling is kinda what Sensei Uchida had in mind."

Morey Uchida was the head of our dojo, our sensei. He had been my teacher for the last seven years and while I'm not someone to indulge in hero worship, I came close to it with my five-foot five-inch instructor. To hear that I needed some schooling of that sort was disconcerting to hear.

"So he had you make sure I saw stars a few time. Guess I did something wrong?"

"No, not in the sense of 'wrong' so much, as Sensei just felt you needed a... course correction."

I looked at him blankly.

"Sensei believes," he went on, "that you've gotten very very good at a few techniques at the expense of being well-rounded. You're damn fast with that side kick, Mac, damn fast, but you rely on it all the time. All. The. Time."

"Oh. It's just that technique's what I have the most success with," I said. Dade smiled. Considering my performance shortly before, I realized how ironic the statement was.

"Sensei wants you to start concentrating more on your upper body attacks and blocks" he continued. "He wants to see more grabbing and grappling. He wanted me to emphasize the point a bit in our little tournament out there, where everyone could benefit from the lesson."

"Okay." But it wasn't really. I rubbed my shoulder, still a little sore from hitting the floor so much. The words I was hearing stung a lot more than the blows to my body. "I see. So, what should I do?"

"Of course, the usual chestnut, 'seek answers in your Kata,' but really, what I want you to do is meet me here for some informal training outside of class once a week. We'll set up a regular time, and maybe I can help you out a bit."

Though I myself had made it to second-degree black belt, being offered a chance to have private time with one of my seniors was pretty damned awesome. Then a realization struck which put a damper on my newfound enthusiasm.

"Er... Sempai? You do know about my odd job situation, don't you?"

"The bounty hunting?"

"Yeah, I often don't know when my Uncle Gil is going to bundle us all into the War Wagon and zoom us all off to God Knows Where in pursuit of some bail-jumping jackass."

"Just let me know when that happens, Mac. Don't have me arrive at the dojo and not know you won't be coming to train. *Wakarimasuka?* For now, just take in the lesson I gave you out on the floor. Don't matter if you're good if you can't stay on your feet."

I rubbed the back of my head. "Don't think I'm gonna forget that one soon, Sempai."

"That's not the main lesson though."

Again, I looked at him blankly.

"The main lesson is," he grinned that big grin, "stop being so predictable, Mac."

CHAPTER THREE

It was a gorgeous summer evening. A loop trail runs the length of my town along both sides of the Columbia River, and it's one of the more scenic attractions the cities of Wenatchee and East Wenatchee have to offer. I had promised myself that even though I was getting a workout at the dojo, I would try to do five miles a night at a good clip. I've found that Karate and related martial arts are good for conditioning, but running (not jogging) brings my ability to move fast to a higher level. Lately, I had won matches with some of my more skilled seniors simply because I became fatigued at a slower pace.

I was crossing the northern bridge and had just reached the east side of the river, when, as commonly happened, the wild area just south of the bridge called to me. I knew I should finish my run, it didn't count for as much if you broke it into pieces, but the setting sun was stunning, and I knew that any animal tracks that were still there would stand out like a carved relief on an ancient Roman building. Had to look.

"You're a weak man, Crow," I said to myself, "Easily led astray. You have to double your speed going back to your wreck of a truck in compensation!" That seemed like a fair trade.

I wandered the short trail through the sage brush and came in through a grove of cottonwoods that helped keep the sandy ground from being returned to the river in flood season. As I walked, I noted the sign of deer, raccoon, and as I slipped down a side trail, I heard a very slight noise above me. I slowly looked up and into the eyes of a

Great Horned Owl, a female by her larger size. She began repetitive sounds deep in her throat that said, "You're stressin' me, boy! Move along so I don't have to!" I dropped my eyes and kept walking, a grin on my face.

I was thrilled to find that the local river otters had visited. Their tracks showed the playful side of their nature and just looking at the nuances of each track made me smile. It was a young pair, playfully chasing each other and their exuberance unfolded in the prints and roll-marks they'd made in the sand. When the prints disappeared back into the river, I decided to sit against a small log and work on my meditation.

Aside from constant encouragement from Sensei to learn to calm my mind, in my younger years I had studied tracking and outdoor skills with the Wilderness Seeker School. The instructors had sent us into the woods for hours at a time, having us sit in a favorite spot repeatedly and that had been the basis of a lot of the awareness skills I had as a tracker. But the woods had always provided something to watch, to learn, to be aware of.

Sensei Uchida wanted me to just sit. Good posture, eyes closed, and do nothing except count my breaths. For someone a month shy of their twenty-fifth birthday, this was possibly the most difficult thing in the world to do. My mind wanted to be constantly chattering.

I wasn't shooting for any kind of world's record at keeping my mind clear, but was starting out (again) at the beginner level, trying to keep my attention on my breathing and ONLY my breathing for ten minutes.

Easy peasy!

About thirty seconds in, I remembered that this month I had barely made the amount my mom and I had agreed upon for a mortgage for my trailer and site. I really hoped that Uncle Gil could find us some--

"Dammit! One.... Two... three..."

I managed to keep counting for what I am sure was a couple of minutes when Rosa's bikini decided to intrude upon my thoughts. Her skin was so smooth and that perfect cinnamon color, and her little muscled butt looked so good in that bikini, and the top, oh man, the top was so skimpy--

"Crap! One... two... three..."

Ok, it was working now, I was really getting along pretty well at this. If I could just keep counting, I was pretty sure I would be able to up my counts to fifteen minutes maybe even a half hour. Finally I was succeeding and Sensei would--

"Frakinations! One... two... three..."

Yeah.

It pretty much went like that for the rest of the sit. I'd be on track, and then my chattering monkey mind would bombard me with thoughts that could've waited 'til later. I managed to do okay for the last few minutes, by counting my breaths in Japanese, forcing me to concentrate on the counting.

"Ichi... Ni... Son..."

For all the difficulties I faced in keeping my mind quiet, I still felt pretty good when I finished. I was calmer and the world seemed just a little bit more... there. I moved up through the nature area, heading south to the large open stretch of beach all the boaters on the Columbia used as a spot to hang out on a hot day. I walked up to the main loop trail and started back the way I had come, when I took a glance at my watch.

"Oh crappola!" I was late, late for a very important date. I began to run, really run.

****

Forty-five minutes later, after a quick shower and change at the dojo I was walking onto Wenatchee Avenue, the main drag in my adopted town. The cool air felt good, as it slowly turned toward the chill of a northern fall night in late September. It was a Wednesday, but the downtown business area had plenty of people out and about. I made my way to the local Vietnamese restaurant and glanced yet again at my watch. Ten minutes late, and it was a miracle that was all.

She was waiting for me and I received that all-knowing eyebrow as she pointedly looked at her watch. Rosa looked VERY good, in a tight medium length black skirt and a black silk-looking top cut just low enough to make a man curious without sending the wrong message. Her makeup was light compared to some women, but she really didn't need much. Hell. With those long eyelashes, she didn't need any.

"Did someone forget they asked someone else out to dinner, Mr. Crow?"

"Someone got caught up with a gorgeous sunset and some otter tracks. Sorry. If you knew how fast I ran to get here and get a shower you might forgive me, just a little." I smiled winningly.

"We shall see, sir. We shall see."

We ordered and I got a tasty beef and tomato dish I could never pronounce and Rosa ordered a shrimp dish that probably wouldn't break my bank. She got a Diet Coke and I went with water. When you order a meal, water's usually free. With the current state of my finances, free was good.

She was not what you'd call a dainty eater. When she was hungry, it was time to eat. While she wasn't uncool about it, she was not about to pick at her meal. It was kind of a pleasure to watch her because it was completely honest. Almost a Zen thing. When eating, eat.

After we were through, I sprang for coffee and we sat and just talked as we liked to do. You always think it'll be only the big events in your life you remember; the vacations, the weddings, birth and deaths. For me, I will always cherish just sitting with her, listening to that throaty laugh, occasionally accidentally touching hands. I hoped we could do it for a long, long time to come.

Eventually, you have to give up the seats though. The waiter had been very patient, and I left him a tip that hurt a bit when Rosa and I walked out on the Ave. Like the ancient song said, we had no particular place to go, and we walked along the street looking in windows and talking about anything that came to mind.

It's good, when you are thinking about someone in a 'more than friends' manner to give the possible relationship the talk test. If you can't keep a conversation going for more than short bursts, you might be barking up the wrong tree. Rosa and I could talk for hours.

Of course, to be honest, I hoped that we might do more than talk, but she insisted on taking it slow this time. Only recently had she even admitted there was something still between us besides friendship.

"You hear anything from your uncle on any new bounties?" she said, pulling us out of the place of walking and flirting and taking us to the place of talking shop. Rosa had bills to pay too.

"He had me doing some research on a guy that skipped out on his bail bondsman over in Snohomish, and I think I might have a lead," I said. "I gave what I had to Uncle Gil. Guess he'll decide if he wants to mobilize us or just keep us working on repairing the ranch house. The pay-off wasn't exactly huge."

"Hope something good turns up soon. I got a car payment next week, and I'm a little short."

"Yeah," I said, "I need to do a little work on the Doom-mobile, but at least I'm gonna make my share of the mortgage payment this month. Hammering and sawing on Uncle Gil's ranch house isn't getting me much more than by."

"Well." She said airily, "You could have kept some of the money from that cache we worked so hard for instead of giving *all* of it to Kailee."

"I felt I needed to," I said. "She was gonna need it." Kailee was a friend who had wound up pregnant by a very evil man. Rosa and I had raided caches left by the god-awful bastard, the son of a rich man, and found a fair amount of cash. I just passed my share on to the one who deserved it more.

"Mac, she has family, and it wasn't your kid."

"Yeah, but I feel better about it, making sure they had a start, at least. That money belonged to the baby's father, after all. Just because he was a rapist and a murderer—well, he wronged Kailee, and that gave her bigger claim to the funds as far as I was concerned. I can sleep better with that."

"See you out at the ranch tomorrow?" Rosa changed the subject. "Work gloves ready for action?"

"I was thinking you might like to come out to my place, and um… watch the river roll by."

She stepped up to me, and put her wrists on my shoulders. She was a good six inches shorter, but sometimes it didn't feel that way.

"That's quite a ways to drive, Mr. Crow. I wouldn't get back to my apartment until very late." She looked up into my face and I could feel her breath on my lips. It was all I could do to keep from shivering like an excited hound dog.

"You don't have to go back to your apartment, you could stay…"

Finger on my lips. "No, we're not back to that stage, you and I, but maybe some day."

"Soon?" I tried hard to not let my voice show anything, but it did crack a little.

"Here's where we are right now." She put her hand behind my head, pulled me down a little and kissed me, long and hard. I've kissed a few girls in my time, but when Rosa kissed me, I felt dizzy, lightheaded. When she pulled away, she seemed a little less sure of her position and was breathing almost as hard as I was.

"Maybe your apartment?"

"No." She smiled up at me. "We agreed, this time we do it slow, sî? Now, let's remember we must be out to the ranch in the morning and go to bed. Separately."

"Okay." I breathed deeply. That of course didn't help the pressure south of my belt buckle one bit.

She ran fingers along my cheek. "Buenas noches, Mac."

"Goodnight."

She walked off to her blue Toyota and I swear to God, she was putting a little extra emphasis on her hips, 'cause I couldn't pull my eyes away until she got in and drove off with a wave.

I really needed a cold shower.

CHAPTER FOUR

When you're low on cash, you have to get creative.

My uncle's fugitive retrieval service had hit slow times for the last several months, and having just paid my share of the mortgage on the property that my mom and I shared, I was getting close to the bone. Breakfast this morning consisted of one egg, the two-day-old remains of a trip to a local Mexican restaurant, the last two sausages and some very watered down orange juice.

Now, all my fridge held was condiments and a few snack items. I still had a fair amount of canned food though. Uncle Gil had been pounding emergency preparedness into my head since I was a teen. Between cans and dehydrated meals, I could eat for quite a while. I guess you could say being out of money was an emergency of sorts.

To be honest, a cup of dry rice, a can of ROTEL, and a can of beans, all poured together and cooked for thirty minutes makes a pretty decent meal. If you can scrounge together some cheese and a can of enchilada sauce, it's a feast. Particularly with a cold beer and a day-old donut. Take that, MacDonald's. I'd rather be able to feed myself any day.

In a small space like my elderly (but lovingly cared for) Airstream trailer, you can't leave things lying around or clutter will drive you nuts. I washed up the two or three dishes I used regularly with a few squirts of Dr. Bronners, made the bed and picked up a few clothes that hadn't made it into the hamper and I was set. When you try not to own much, you don't have to take care of much.

I decided to take some outdoor time before I went out to Uncle

Gil's farmhouse to help with repairs. I'm an early riser, and there was plenty of time until I needed to hit the road. I was enjoying the cool air on the small deck I had made, when the sun had just cleared the basalt cliffs to the east. The early sunlight felt good on my bare shoulders.

Putting on an old pair of running shoes and grabbing my old canvas fanny pack, I wandered down the 100 feet to the edge of the Columbia River. I saw that the local great blue heron had been by to thin the number of unwary fish along my stretch of shoreline. His tracks were deep in the mud, like a small dinosaur's.

Looking around to see that no one else was going to be observing my madness, I waded in. When the water hit a certain spot below the belt line, I stifled a gasp.

"Where were you last night when I needed you?" I grumbled.

I carefully bowed to the east, and took the ready stance, the *kamae*, of my martial arts system. Tensing my muscles, I brought my arms up into a doubled chamber and began the dynamic tension/breathing form named Sanchin. It's sort of the opposite of Tai Chi, in that the muscles are kept tense through almost the entire exercise while the breath is forced down into the abdomen by partially closing the throat.

Yeah. If you're not training in Karate, it looks pretty damn strange. It's not a form I go out and perform in the local park.

Standing in water up to my belly button that had come straight off the glaciers of the Cascade mountains, it was all I could do not to rush, which was part of the training. The cold was meant to be a distraction to overcome. I kept my concentration, for the most part, but it was all I could do to not rush out of the frigid water when I was done.

"What the heck…" As I headed back for the house, I saw coyote tracks, very fresh ones, heading down the dirt road by my home. Tracks always have my attention, and I noted the outside toe on the right rear track bent out at almost a forty-five degree angle from the paw. The track was very large for a coyote.

"That sure looks familiar." It was a bit of a mystery, and I wanted to follow the trail. A mystery is the surest bait you can use when a tracker is involved.

But I had promises to keep, and miles to drive to keep them.

****

It was finally getting to be less of a toss-up whether the Doom-mobile would start or not. I had purchased the old Ford Ranger last year after my beloved 4-Runner had met an explosive end and it had taken the last of my reserve funds to keep it running. The upside was that I learned a lot about working on cars, thanks to my friend and fellow bounty hunter, Vinny. The downside had been that the hulk had taken a lot more TLC to get it running faithfully than I would have guessed when buying it at Bill's used cars.

Once you got it started, it ran pretty good, and the hour and a half drive to my uncle's farmstead went by without mechanical mishap. I drove up the long driveway to the old farmhouse being renovated due to events earlier in the year, but as I turned off the old truck, it tried to keep chugging through a few more cycles. I gave it a stern look. It finally quit.

"Well," a voice said, "decided to finally grace us with yer presence, have ya?"

"Really?" I replied, smiling, "A whopping ten minutes late and this is the reception I get?"

"Being on time for a job builds character, young Mac." Ed Burnbaum, hobbled up on his single cane. His grin was wide.

"This from the guy who left society behind and went to live in the woods for twenty years?"

"Worked out well for you, didn't it?"

It had indeed. Ed had become my wilderness mentor as a teen, and when his deep forest cabin had been destroyed, he'd come east to my uncle's farm to be caretaker. He'd traded Pacific rainforest for sagebrush desert, but the change seemed to suit him. He was seventy years old, a Viet Nam vet, and one of the best teachers I'd ever had. My ability to follow tracks over difficult surfaces had flourished under his teaching.

"Yes, yes it did. So where are we on the repair schedule today?"

Ed squinted at the house. "Vinnie and I took down all the bullet-holed drywall yesterday. I'll have you pull off the siding from the outside and we'll see if we've got any structural damage to the house that'll need fixin'. I know for a fact there's a couple of power feeds in there that I had to shut the breakers off for, so there might be other problems. I got Rosa inside, pulling off the paneling near the fireplace. More than a few splintered pieces there."

I picked up a pry bar from a pile of tools under the eaves of the porch and began to pry fifty-year-old boards off the front of the house. The boards looked like worm wood with all the bullet holes in them. It was hard to look at.

"Those bastards sent quite a few rounds our way," Ed observed.

"For guys who were supposed to kidnap Kailee, they sure put her in harm's way."

"Yes, but they paid, Mac. They paid. Glad your uncle had all this stonework put in at the base o' the house. Gave everyone a little room to keep their heads down. Oh! Hey! Guess who I saw saunter by this morning?"

"Him?"

"Yep. His lordship went loping by with a chukar in his mouth. Looked over at me while I was drinkin' my coffee out here and just didn't have the slightest worry at all about me. Didn't give a damn. He's got that big ol' scar on that left flank, like you said."

"That is the weirdest dang coyote I've ever seen."

"The King's got an attitude, to be sure. Went right across the driveway there."

Something surfaced from the back of my mind, and I went out to the driveway and looked for the tracks of the scruffy big *canis latrans*. I found them quickly, and what I saw made me wonder.

"Hey, Ed! Can you come take a look at this?" He hobbled up, and I pointed. "Look at this right rear paw here. The outter toe."

"Yep. We've seen that toe sticking' out every time we've tracked the old bugger."

"I was out this morning, at my place, and I found a track exactly like this one. Same foot, same toe variance."

"Interesting!"

"Seriously, if you had put that track from this morning in this trail we're looking at, I wouldn't be able to tell the difference."

Ed looked at me then. He had continued my training after I'd been booted from the Seeker School, and he knew I was hard to fool when it came to tracking. He had certainly tried often enough.

"Well, young MacKenzie," he said thoughtfully, "so you think this ol' coyote is so enamored of yer company that he followed you forty miles, swam a mile-wide river and laid them tracks down so you'd know he was thinkin' of you?"

"Ha! Kinda doubt that." Ed has a way of pointing out a person's absurdities and getting that person to laugh at the same time. We were interrupted by my phone emitting a particularly obnoxious ringtone, a harsh red-alert sound. It was a tone I had reserved specially.

"Hello, Uncle Gil."

"MacKenzie? I need your particular skill set at the office, pronto."

"The guy from Snohomish?"

"Better. A local boy, suspected of murder and fraud but out on bail. Which he has skipped big time. So drop what you're doing, and help me figure out where he might be."

"Ok, I just need to get the tarps up on the front of the house, and I'll head in."

"Chop-chop. Daylight's a-burnin'."

CHAPTER FIVE

I pulled up to our office in Wenatchee with a new coat of dust on the Doom-mobile. The backroads of eastern Washington state are notorious for a fine powdery dust that causes many people who live along them to not wash their cars often. Why bother?

Our office was just as pedestrian looking as my dusty pickup. My uncle believes in keeping a low profile in every aspect of his life, going with the thought that the less people know about you, the less they will interfere with you. Especially the U.S. government, for which he has a particular lack of warmth.

I walked in the door, and my uncle, Gil Chambers, sat hunched over a laptop, trying mightily to force the "infernal machine" to do his bidding. Aligned in a neat set of rows beside it were the various pieces of paperwork a "fugitive retrieval specialist" must have to do the job without going to jail.

"Hello," I said, "I'm from the government, and I'm here to help."

"Very funny, kiddo," he replied. "That kind of help almost no one needs."

My uncle is a craggy-faced ex-military man, and I used to think he had no sense of humor. Now I know it's just so dry that most mere mortals can't get the joke.

"So whatcha got for me?" I asked, looking at the open laptop. I saw a sad-eyed dark-haired man with a serious five-o'clock shadow.

"Elizondo Gutierrez. Suspected in the death of two men found in a field near Arlington, both known associates of this guy. Case was circumstantial enough that the judge set a bail, a pretty high one," Uncle Gil replied. "Gutierrez got Overguard Bail Services to bankroll his bail, if you can believe that."

"Overguard? They're usually pretty conservative about huge bails…"

"Elizondo here somehow got them to accept a house near Seattle as collateral. Showed them pretty photos, and when they ran a background check, the records showed he was the owner. But no one ever actually drove out there and took a look at it before agreeing to cover his bail."

"Oh, shit."

"Yep. There was a house there, if you wanted to be charitable with the term house, but the masses of blackberries growing out the front door tended to devalue it a bit. That, and the eight inches of moss on the half collapsed roof."

"The land?"

"Worth about half what they're on the hook for bail."

I thought about it for a moment. "Doesn't Overguard have their own agents to track this dude down?"

"Why do you think they shunted it to us, son? Guess how long 'til the trial?"

"Oh no." I was sure the answer was not going to be good.

"Yep. Three days. And then the judge is going to order that bail money forfeit and Overguard will take a very big hit. Tim's had his guys and gals on it for the last two weeks." He gestured to a pile of reports. "They've checked with every relative, every friend, every fool he hangs with. Nada."

"So what are we gonna do that they haven't?"

"We need to take a stab it, because the stakes are pretty sizable. We're running way lean as it is and if we can pull it off, we could go a couple more slow months without any problems."

"How much?" I asked. My uncle told me, and I immediately became more enthusiastic about the whole thing.

"Okay then! Where do we start?"

"You start by reading all their reports, and find what they've missed, young Jedi. The rest of us will be here to bounce your ideas off of."

"Wait. What? I'm supposed to be the one finding him?"

"Vinnie, Rosa, and myself got nuttin'. If anyone can pull an idea out of their ass, it's you."

I just stared at him, mouth open. Uncle Gil's lopsided smile appeared, frightening small children for miles around.

"You'll find him, son. You're a tracker, right? So... track, Mac."

****

It wasn't as awful as it seemed.

I don't think anyone is going to say reading footprints and sign on the ground is the same as electronically searching for a fugitive, but there's still a similar method to both. You have to read, by what your quarry has left behind, the path that they've taken.

Though I might've given Uncle Gil a little attitude, the truth was, I enjoyed the challenge. I also enjoyed that I was beginning to be the go-to guy when it came to figuring out where our bail welcher might go. This was in sharp contrast to last year, when I felt like Johnny Tag-a-long, only there because I was the owner's nephew.

As the others in our little group prepped equipment and took care of details, I furiously searched through databases. "Hey, look at this!" I said as Rosa walked past. She stopped and pulled the chair up beside me and looked at the screen.

"Not the first time our boy had been arrested and taken to trial," she said.

"No, this arrest was for being part of an email scamming group. They all got off because they were good at covering their tracks, and the prosecutors couldn't make the charges stick. Look at the people arrested with him though, particularly the woman."

"Irena Rochenko," Rosa said, looking at the JPEG of the woman's mug shot. "Pretty, but there's a hardness to her eyes. 'Course she's being mug shotted at the time. That doesn't sit well with anyone."

"Ah, but here's the thing. The folks at Overguard have been muddying the waters over on the west side of the state and came up with nada. Guess where Irena lives."

"Not on the west side?"

"She has a home in one of the fancy gated communities..." I paused for effect, "..at Lake Chelan."

Rosa's grin started out small and slowly grew into a big dazzling smile.

"Yep," I said. "If I wanted to get away from my usual stomping grounds, what better place to hide than in a secure luxury golf course community, in a faraway tourist destination?"

"Chelan's just forty-five minutes upriver. Wouldn't cost us much to check on it."

"I'll tell Uncle Gil and Vinnie."

****

"Hell, we may as well, Gil. Those dinglebrains at Overguard have already stomped a mud hole in the places we would normally have looked, and it costs the company very little to actually go just up the road," Vinnie, our second in command said. "Hell, if nothin' else, it'll be a nice dry run to not let our skill sets rust."

Vincent 'Vinnie' Lugar was half owner of the company, though several years younger than my uncle. He looked like a tow-headed Iowa farm boy, but he was a professional soldier through and through.

He also had one asset I didn't possess. My uncle would listen to him.

They (and Rosa for that matter) had all seen military service, and I hadn't. This contributed to the problem of my needing extra help when trying to get a cogent point across to Uncle Gil.

"This case you were looking at, it's almost ten years old. I had a friend check the lady in question and she's had no brushes with the law since this escapade. Gutierrez, on the other hand, seems like a trouble magnet, and she'd be wise to keep clear of him." Uncle Gil rumbled.

"Let's all be honest here, how often do people involved in this stuff make a wise decision?" Vinnie asked.

"Gil," Rosa cut in, "we can do this without much effort or cost outlay. We're in our own county, and the authorities know us so we don't have to worry about friction with the LEOs. What can it hurt to check?"

I wanted to chime in that I thought it was a pretty solid lead, however, as I get older I am slowly (very slowly) learning to keep my mouth shut. If I started pushing, the ol' man might start balking just because I thought it was a good idea.

I could resent that, or I could learn to work with it. I kept my mouth shut.

Uncle Gil sat thoughtfully for a moment, then, looking around at all of us said. "All right. We're green. Load up."

CHAPTER SIX

The small resort town of Chelan is on one of the deepest and longest lakes in the United States. Lake Chelan is around 50 miles long, a good portion of which lies in national forest land. Much of the rest of the area has been bought up by Microsoft managers and wealthy retirees from all points across the nation. Needless to say, the number one source of employment for the locals is tourism.

We had driven up the usually scenic drive on the west side of the Columbia River in a dense, wet fog. During the entire trip, Vinnie was on the phone putting things into place. The first call had been to the small police force of the city of Chelan to let them know we were operating in their territory, though technically, we were outside the city limits.

"Understood. We won't likely be comin' into Chelan."

I couldn't hear what was being said on the other end of the line, but from Vinnie's expression, I guessed it was probably none too friendly.

"So I'd guess you guys wouldn't be interested in helping us out with an officer on location, would you?" Vinnie asked. "Always nice to have one of our law enforcement officials on… ah. Outside your jurisdiction. I see. Ok, thanks. Yep. We'll try not to bring any trouble into town. Bye."

"Not willing to give us the time of day, I'd guess," Rosa said.

"Got that right, l'il sis. Let's see if the county sheriff might be in the market for a little supervisory over watch action."

"They'll help if they can," Uncle Gil said from the driver's seat. "We've done enough extra for them helping out during fire season, we've got a decent rapport."

While Vinnie keyed into a special line to the actual Sheriff of Chelan County, I nudged Rosa and said quietly enough so my uncle wouldn't hear.

"I hope this pans out. It's hard enough to get him to trust my judgement as it is." My uncle and I had an odd relationship. He sometimes had a hell of a time believing that I was an adult.

"Maybe," she said, "but this time he asked you to help him find a lead. That's new. So you provided one, which is more than Vinnie and I together could do. If it don't pan out, not much lost, and we get to practice. Where's the down side?"

"The down side would be if he gives me… The Look, then shakes his head."

She grinned at me. For some time, Rosa has watched the mini-war between my uncle and me, a never ending battle to show that I could measure up.

"If he does, practice your fancy Zen 'letting go' exercises. Like you said, everything is a chance to practice."

"Yeah."

"Outstanding!" Vinnie said, loud enough we all looked at him. "That's great. We'll meet deputy Mathews at the gate. Maybe having him with us will make it easier to get past security for the community. Thanks! We appreciate it."

"Sounds like we might have some help," Uncle Gil said.

"We got an officer to back us up." Vinnie agreed. "Never underestimate the power of being helpful."

****

Driving down the long hill that headed toward the lake, we saw the sign for the golf community on our left. It was hard to miss. You can usually tell if a place is for the wealthy by the entrance signage. The sign here was so impressive that it probably cost more than the trailer I live in. When you have a waterfall at your entrance sign, you know that everything is going to involve big money.

We drove up the hilly driveway to a well-maintained security gate and Uncle Gil gestured for Vinnie to go and make contact with the security guard there.

"You two kids go with Vinnie and listen." He gestured for Rosa and me to follow. "You both got things to learn about dealing with bureaucrats, and Vinnie's the team charmer. Just give him a little space to work, and try not to look intimidating."

"So, now *I'm* a kid?" Rosa said, as we walked toward the gate. "I'm not sure I like being lumped in with riff raff like you."

"You are only three and a half years older."

"Is not the years, baby, it's da the mileage."

"Okay, Indiana Jones."

We approached the gate, and could see without much effort, that our team charmer was having trouble.

"Look, buddy," Vinnie said, "We're not here to kick down doors or to cause your residents any trouble. This dude we're looking for is implicated in two murders. If he's here, and we can find and remove him, then all the people who live here will be a lot safer. The guy is bad news on several fronts."

"Oh no," the guard said. "I'm not letting a bunch of crazy-ass mercenaries go careening through this place. Are you nuts?" The guard was almost as big as Vinnie, and surprisingly, for a security guard, looked in pretty good shape. "I've seen the show where those bounty hunters go wild running people down. Screw that!"

As our entire team silently cursed 'reality' TV, a Chelan County Sheriff's patrol car drove up. Most of the smaller towns in the area contracted with the county sheriff to provide police services they couldn't afford to bankroll themselves. The sheriff's department here carried a good reputation, and that reputation tended to carry a lot of weight.

The deputy got out of his car and walked over. "Hello, would you be Mister Chambers?"

"No, I'm his partner, Vinnie Lugar. Deputy Mathews?"

"Yep. I understand you need a little backup on a runner?"

"It always goes more smoothly when we have a little LEO backup. I appreciate the help."

"The sheriff seems to think well of you folks. So, we ready to do this?"

"Having a little difficulty convincing this gentleman to let us pass."

The deputy walked over and began a conversation with the guard.

"We need to get in there, sir."

"Look, officer. It's my job to keep trouble out of this development, and these bounty hunters look like nuthin' but trouble to me," the guard said.

"If they're wrong, they'll be out of here quickly. I guarantee it," Mathews replied. "But if they're right, you already have trouble. I did a quick check on the dude they're tracking, and I'm telling you, you do not want him anywhere near the people you supply security for."

Had it been only our team making the request, I think he would have balked. With the added weight of a 'legitimate' law enforcement officer, the security guard caved. He opened the gate and waved us through with a disgusted look on his face.

"Pequeño bebé. Muy triste." *Poor baby. So Sad.* Rosa shook her head in disgust. "People could die and he's worried that someone might be inconvenienced. Estúpido."

"Death can be pretty inconvenient," I said.

"There's an old saying: let no new thing arise," Uncle Gil told her "and we are certainly in that category."

"Am I hearing things or are you taking up for that brain-dead fish, Gilbert?" Rosa said. "He should be thanking us."

"Not on your life. Just attempting to understand the ignorant," Uncle Gil's low voice rumbled. "It makes it easier to navigate the job."

"Sî," she agreed.

"Wow. Look at this place," I said. "Manicured to the Nth degree."

"What did you expect? This is where the very well paid wind up, not hard scrabblers like us," Vinnie laughed. "This is 'the other house' for administrators, lawyers, CEOs and such. Heh, if you work really hard you can live here too someday, Mac." Vinnie laughed, perhaps enjoying the joke a bit too much. "I'll bet these houses actually have bathrooms – unlike your trailer."

"Too much luxury for me," I muttered, the sight of these mansions built so close together somewhat nauseating. "I'd feel like a frickin' bird in a cage. And anyway, I have a spa bathroom. It's just fifty feet away from the trailer."

"It's true. He even has scented soap. It stinks for sure, but it does have a scent." Unlike me, Rosa seemed in awe of the beautiful homes, her head in continual spinning motion.

"Makes me wonder how this woman we're going to visit funded her place here," she said.

"She wasn't convicted of theft. Maybe she just got away with it," I said.

"Then internet fraud must pay well," She replied. "I wonder how hard it would be to fake a Nigerian IP address and tell the gullible that you have money for them."

"Or tell the lonely how much you love them," I growled.

We passed several clumps of homes, all easily in the million dollar range, and I was surprised to see the developers had left picturesque bits of sagebrush land between the clusters of huge houses. As we followed the winding road deeper in, Deputy Mathew's cruiser followed closely.

We found the house number on a mailbox at the bottom of long up-sloping driveway with an older white SUV parked at the top. Uncle Gil pulled the War Wagon over just to the South of the entrance, and the deputy pulled up alongside.

"This the address?" he asked. Uncle Gil nodded. "Okay, then."

The deputy parked his car across the base of the driveway, and we all smiled. We couldn't legally get away with that, but no one could tell a law officer where to park. We all assembled at the foot of the drive and began putting on vests.

"I'll hang back down here," the deputy told us. "Sheriff said only to get involved if there was a crime committed."

"I could give you one of our radios, if you'd care to monitor the situation," Vinnie told him.

"I guess that wouldn't be too directly involved." Mathews took the radio.

We spread out and approached the SUV. I noted the plate, and radioed it to Mathews, in case he wanted to run it through the DMV.

"The SUV's pretty beat up, doesn't match the surroundings," Rosa said. It gave me hope that the vehicle belonged to Gutierrez. When I peeked around the back left corner, I saw the driver's side door was open and as Rosa came up she pointed out the keys were dangling from the ignition, with a little Lego Darth Vader on a chain dangling from the keys.

Darth is still swinging slightly.

Rosa looked at me, looked at the ground and back at me.

I dropped down into a crouch as Vinnie came around the SUV and Rosa stopped him by raising her forefinger in his direction. He saw what I was doing and froze.

The fog had been heavy here too, and getting down low, I could see tracks on the asphalt, places that the condensation had been scraped off as someone walked toward the truck. The tracks came to the driver's side, and were meshed with Rosa's and my own tracks, but a careful look around showed the trail went off the opposite bank of the driveway.

The side that was blocked from our view as we drove up.

"Whatcha got, son?" Uncle Gil asked.

"Somebody went over the bank here, just as we were driving up, I'd say."

"You sure?"

"Yes, sir. Here's one of his prints." I pointed to a spot off the asphalt where the edge of some running shoe tread shown. As we watched, some of the bunch grass that had been mashed down sprung back up. It doesn't get much fresher than that.

"Gil!" Rosa yelled, "over there!"

We all looked where she pointed, and below us on the lush green golf course, a figure was running all out towards the pines on the edge of the fairway. Uncle Gil held down the transmit button on his radio so that Mathews could listen in.

"Rosa, you and Vinnie, after him. Make sure of his identity before you make an arrest. Officer Mathews? Evidently our guy saw us coming and is in flight north toward the lake. We are pursuing."

"Be advised, that SUV is indeed Mr. Gutierrezz's," Mathews replied over the radio.

"What about me?" I asked as my team mates went bounding down the hill.

"Mac, I want you to gain entrance to the house, legally. I have a bad feeling..." He looked at the lavish structure and then pointed to a duffle that sat in the passenger seat of the SUV. "Check that. I'm going to see if I can head Elizondo off in the War Wagon."

Once again, I had been kept from direct action. It chafed, but this was not the time to complain about it, and as he trotted down the drive, I opened the passenger door, unzipped the duffle and peeked inside.

I had never before in my life seen that much cash.

There were some twenties, some hundreds but it was mostly fifties. A lot of fifties.

No, I mean a LOT of fifties.

For a second I thought about all the bills I had waiting for me at home, then I firmly bitchslapped that part of my mind. I've got ancestors watching somewhere. I didn't want to have to explain myself to them someday.

"Deputy Mathews, this is Mac Crow at the SUV. There is a ton of cash in a duffle here. Something is definitely not kosher."

"I'm coming up."

As he walked up the drive, I pointed towards the passenger seat and started toward the front door of the house.

"I'm gonna see if I can get anyone to answer the door and let me in." I told him.

"I can't go in without a warrant, Mr. Crow," he said while glancing in at the open duffle, "If you see any evidence of a crime and you report it, I can come in and join you."

Cops couldn't enter a home without a warrant or strong probable cause, however they were a lot better insulated against legal action than my profession. We were all going to be careful and by the book.

I knocked on the heavy front door, and it swung in on its own, almost never a good sign. It did, however, give me an excuse to enter.

"Hello! Is there anybody home? Your front door is open. Is anyone injured in here?"

I thought I heard a groan from upstairs, but it was very faint. It was enough though to give me reason to enter. I carefully stepped in, hand on the butt of my Glock, ready to get it out of the retention system holster as quickly as I could.

The interior would have been a shoe-in for HGTV. Stylish art sculptures lined the walls, and a gigantic fireplace sat in a room with huge windows looking down at the lake. I heard that faint groan again. Definitely upstairs.

"Hello!" I called out as I went up the ornate spiral staircase. "Where are you? Do you need help?"

I came into the master bedroom and she lay there on the floor, in the middle of an ocean of bloody blue carpet. Irena Rochenko looked up at me weakly and raised her hand as if to plead for help.

"Team! This is Mac. Gutierrez is armed. I have a gunshot victim in the house. Deputy Mathews, can you get an ambulance on the way and join me? I need help here!"

"Copy!" Both Uncle Gil and Mathews said at the same time. I heard my uncle giving instructions to Rosa and Vinnie, but couldn't listen too closely. I had my personal trauma bandage out, along with the latex gloves we all carry, and was trying to plug one of Irena's bleeding wounds. I yanked a pillowcase off of a pillow on the bed and began attempting to quell blood flowing from the other wound in her stomach as best I could. Trying to keep pressure on two bleeding wounds at the same time is about as easy as it sounds.

"Irena? Can you hear me?" She opened her eyes. "Help is on the way, you've just got to hang in there!"

She closed her eyes again, and my heart rate jumped. I needed to keep her awake.

"Irena! Don't go to sleep on me now! Keep those eyes open." I heard a noise behind me and saw Mathews carrying a big first aid kit.

"Ambulance is on its way," he said. He pulled the blood soaked pillowcase off and replaced it with a fresh trauma bandage. "Keep her talking, Mac."

"Irena! Keep your eyes open for me. Did Elizondo do this to you? Is he the one who shot you? Talk to me."

She opened her eyes again and looked into mine. "Su'…bitch found my money. Said… needed it… move to Canada… all I had." Her voice was faint, one of the bullets had surely punctured a lung.

"He shot you for the money?"

"Yes!" She broke into pained tears. "Elizondo took it all… then shot me. Thought he killed me."

I looked up at Mathews and he returned my look, grim and angry.

Elizondo Gutierrez was sure as shit not going to get bail this time.

I did my best to keep her conscious, but she kept drifting in and out. After about twenty minutes, we heard sirens and shortly thereafter, I was able to step away and let the EMTs take over. After helping them get the gurney down the stairs with Irena on it, I stepped out into the driveway and noted the duffle was still there. I zipped it shut, and took it down to Mathews.

"You'll probably want to take charge of this," I said.

"Yep. Probably be for the best, I..." The radio interrupted him.

"Mac! We got him. We're returning to the house to pick you up," my uncle's voice blared out of the tiny speaker. "How's the victim?"

"She's on her way to the hospital, in bad shape. I'm hoping she'll make it there."

"I copy that. Be there in ten minutes. Out."

"May be some jurisdiction problems here. I'm gonna have to talk to my bosses before I can let you take this guy anywhere," Mathews said.

"The existing bench warrant for a murder case will get first crack at him, I think, but I'll let my uncle sort that stuff out with you."

"I was meaning to ask you, how'd you guys know he went towards the golf course?" the deputy asked. "He must've seen us coming, and hightailed it before you all got up to that SUV."

"Keys were in the door, so he probably hadn't been there long before. I just dropped down low, and his tracks stood out in the moisture of the driveway." I said. "It was pretty easy, compared to some of the places I've had to track at."

"Wait. You're the guy," he said looking at me as if with some great revelation. "You tracked that little girl on the west side, right? Then you found the psycho that was after her! That was you, wasn't it?"

"Well, yeah. That was me." There was so much more to that story that I didn't want to get in to. Stuff I didn't even want to remember.

"Holy shit. You do any tracking for hire?"

"I actually tracked down two lost people previously in conjunction with your own department."

"Wait, the guy at Lake Wenatchee? That was you? Aw, sorry. An organization gets big enough and covers enough territory, the right hand often doesn't know what the left hand is up to."

"I did that as a volunteer, but I'm always looking for paying work," I said. "Why? You lose someone?"

"Ever heard of Loman County?"

"Um… isn't that the small county west of Okanogan County? The one that's eighty percent federal wilderness area?"

"That's it. They've got a fugitive that's gone deep into that wilderness, and they reached out to us to see if we had a tracker on staff. Needless to say, with our budget that sort of thing is pretty much done by freelancers or volunteers."

"How well I know that." I'd been trying to get some paid work of out of my local sheriff's department, but the only type of tracking that had come up was lost hiker tracking. That was always volunteer Search and Rescue. Evidently, no criminals in our area had the hutzpah to try to Rambo it out in the wild.

"You have a card or anything?"

"Here's our company card," I said, handing him one. "They can contact me through my uncle."

"Okay, Mac Crow. Let me see if I can get you a job!"

CHAPTER SEVEN

As I expected, Uncle Gil got the last word on custody of the prisoner. We were en route to a meeting with Overguard Bail Services at the top of Stevens Pass, a nice midway meeting point to make the hand off. Elizondo Gutierrez sat between Vinnie and Uncle Gil, both of whom were large and imposing gentlemen. Intimidation was not something we were adverse to using in our line of work.

Our runner was a medium-sized man, and as we drove the lengthy course of Highway 2, he began to enumerate the reasons why he was innocent and we should let him go.

"Honest, you guys know this is just a misunderstanding! I never killed no one. Someone has it in for me, probably that guy at Overguard. He just wants to get my house, so he's makin' it look like I ran out, but I never did. Hell, my hearing is a few days from now, I was gonna be there!" he whined.

Both Vinnie and Uncle Gil are men of action and experience. Rosa has seen her share of crap too. They've probably all heard statements like this hundreds of times. I, on the other hand, have not quite learned the art of not letting myself be baited. I felt my temper flare.

"Dude! Seriously?" I growled. "You had the gun in your possession. Ballistics will prove that same gun shot poor Irena. You pulled that same weapon on two of my friends here and you think ANYONE in this vehicle is going to take your side?"

"MacKenzie," Uncle Gil said mildly.

"Not to mention the firearm you were carrying was a violation of your bail contract *and* it had all the serial numbers filed off!" I guess my voice was getting louder, because I felt a vice-like grip on my shoulder. I looked at my uncle's craggy face, he ever so slightly shook his head.

I sat back in my seat, almost shaking with anger at our prisoner. The others hadn't been there while Irena's blood had been leaking all over the carpet.

"Don't worry, Mac," Rosa said from the driver's seat, "Ol' Elizondo there has pretty much screwed up any chance his lawyer had of an acquittal. He'll go into court, and if he can't get a plea deal, which at this late date I doubt will even be on the table, he'll wind up in a cell waiting for his next trial for today's little outburst."

"Rosa," Uncle Gil said mildly. Rosa is a faster study than I, she buttoned it.

"Fuck you!" Elizondo was not a fast study. "When I need the opinion of some little whore..." His words turned into a stream of insults in Spanish, which I could barely keep up with.

His voice cut off suddenly, rising to a high squeak before going silent. I covertly looked back and saw that my uncle had our prisoner's earlobe tightly squeezed between thumb and forefinger. He slowly brought Elizondo's head around so their noses were about an inch apart.

"Manners," Uncle Gil said, staring the man directly in the eyes.

Gutierrez had nothing more to say for the rest of the trip.

****

Stevens Pass is a very popular ski area during the winter time. It's fairly breathtaking in the fall as well, with amazing colors and steep hillsides rife with waterfalls. The grandeur seemed wasted on Elizondo.

We pulled into the parking lot for the almost deserted ski area and saw a large black GMC Yukon SUV parked there. As we rolled to a stop, Tim Moriano stepped out of the Yukon, along with two of his agents, huge men, neither of which I knew. Tim had been in the business for years, and had helped my uncle start his own business. He was a gray-haired man of indeterminate age, but unlike many of the people we worked with, he kept in shape. Good shape.

"Gil!" he said warmly, "Been too long. Looks like you've done me a real favor here."

"Tim. Good to see you too."

"And damn, is this Mac? Sheesh, boy! You went and got big. I see Gil's roped you into the family biz. Better run, son. It's an addictive occupation."

"Too late, Mr. Moriano," I said, "I'm already hooked."

He shook his head with mock gravitas. "And this must be Ms. Fernandez?"

"Please, call me Rosa," she said.

We might've gone on with small talk, but Vinnie had pulled Gutierrez from our SUV and Moriano's focus went to him like a laser.

"Elizondo! Do I need to enumerate the ways in which I am disappointed in you?"

Gutierrez didn't answer, looking defiantly at us all. As Vinnie stepped behind him to encourage him to move forward, our prisoner threw his entire body backwards, colliding with Vinnie. The parking lot was slick with rain and even though Vinnie was twice Elizondo's size, he lost his footing and went down.

Our fugitive was off like a shot.

It was stupid of course. His hands were still zip-tied behind him, and he was running like a spastic cow, to God only knows where. The ski resort is in the center of a national forest, surrounded by nothing but wilderness for miles and miles.

My uncle looked over at me and said in the mildest of tones, "MacKenzie, would you mind?"

I was off like a shot, admittedly grinning at the opportunity to knock Gutierrez on his ass. I heard footsteps running beside me.

"Race you!" Rosa yelled, and we were off.

"Oh no you don't!"

Oh yes she did. I'm six-foot-two, and Rosa is five-foot-seven. We both strive to keep in shape, a requirement of a business where you often wind up in foot races with fleeing felons, but pure physics dictated that my longer legs should have left her behind.

She pulled out ahead.

"Elizondo!" she yelled and with the finesse of a jujitsu master she kicked Gutierrez's right foot slightly to the left as it came off the ground. His right instep hooked his left heel, and he went down like the proverbial sack of potatoes. The icing on the cake was that he landed in a puddle, a deep one and by the time we wrestled him to his feet, he was soaked to the skin. No one felt sorry for him.

The two big guys took him from us and I said, "Sorry about the mess."

"Don't worry about it. Having this guy back is gonna make all our lives better," the big blond guy said. Neither of them introduced themselves, but it didn't bother me. As long as Tim sent us a nice big check, they could be as taciturn as they wanted.

Rosa and I walked back to Uncle Gil as Moriano was handing him an unsealed envelope. "As we agreed, Gil. With a bit extra for a quick recovery. Just send me a receipt. With this deal, I'm able to afford to be generous."

"Oh?" Uncle Gil asked.

"Oh, yeah. The only way I'd take Elizondo on was if we put a clause in our contract that his collateral would become mine if he skipped. I'll not only *not* lose my money, but that piece of crap house and land that he owns now reverts to me. I'm pretty sure if I demolish the place, I can get a builder to buy it at a premium price. When I said you done me a real favor, I wasn't just makin' conversation. I believe in passing some of the good fortune on."

"Thanks Tim. Things have been a little lean lately. This'll definitely stimulate our economy."

"De nada. See you all later."

The Yukon pulled out of the parking lot and headed down the west side of the pass. We climbed into the War Wagon and Uncle Gil said from the driver's seat: "I'm thinkin' a stop in Leavenworth. Anyone interested in landing at the Icicle Brewing Company? I'm buying."

Oddly enough, there was not one protest.

CHAPTER EIGHT

The next day, I was back out at Uncle Gil's farm, nailing siding to the front of the house. Though I now had a little money, I had committed to helping with this project, and a man's got to honor his commitments. Rosa was also there, helping Ed and I shift the boards up into position so I could hit them with the nail gun. Rosa lived up to her commitments too.

"Well," Ed Burnbaum said, "That's lookin' pretty good! A little paint and you'd hardly know we had a running gun battle out here."

"Gonna be tough to match the paint from the old boards," Rosa noted.

"Welp, we might just have to paint the whole shebang then," Ed said. Rosa and I both groaned. "Besides, if I know your uncle, we'd probably better start lookin' for some camouflage house paint."

We were all still grinning when the man, himself, came out of the house.

"Mac, Rosa, I've direct deposited your wages into your accounts," Uncle Gil told us. "The usual ten percent has been taken out and put in the IRAs I started for you."

"Oh, that's good, 'cause my check is so huge, I won't even miss ten percent," Rosa said, dryly.

"You won't be so snippy someday, when you're older than I am and compound interest has made you one of the few people in your age bracket that has money," he grumbled, "Most people around here today ain't puttin' anything into their retirement, thinkin' that Social Security will take care of 'em when they get old."

"Oh shit, Rosa, you pushed the button," I said. "You pushed the button!" Rosa looked at me in mock horror. She knew exactly what was coming and it was too late to stop it.

"Damn fools," Uncle Gil went on, "they think that the corrupt bastards we have in congress and the senate will be able to restrain themselves from stealing all that Social Security money, just lying there for them to pilfer. 'Course the whole reason Social Security's in such a financial mess now is because the damn politicians couldn't keep their greedy lunch hooks out of it in the first place. Quite frankly, I think they'll destroy it before I make it to retirement age, much less when you two manage…"

About eight minutes in, Ed saved the day.

"Gil, I'm sure you're right about alla that stuff, there, but these youngsters been workin' hard gettin' yer place put back together. Can we getcha to take a look at it then?"

He sized up the new siding. "Looks a hell of a lot better than it did, last week. Good job. Now what were you sayin' about paint? Honestly, the whole place looks like it was painted ten years before I even bid on the foreclosure. Yeah. I'd like to see it all stripped and repainted."

"Oh, lord, do we have to strip and sand it first?" I groaned. "Can't we just go over the old paint?"

Ed and Uncle Gil both looked at me like I had suggested wearing dog poop covered shoes to go across the living room carpet. I was saved when my uncle's phone started chiming in his pocket.

"Yeah. This is Chambers. She is?" he said. "That's good news, especially for her. Yeah. I'll tell my nephew. Really? Well, isn't that something. I'll be awaiting their call."

Putting his phone down, Uncle Gil told us, "Evidently, Ms. Rochenko survived. That was someone from the sheriff's department. Said that without Mac's help here, she probably would have bled out."

Was it my imagination, or was their just the tiniest hint of pride in his voice?

Probably just my imagination.

He started to say more, but his phone again chimed and he put it to his ear.

"Yes, this is he," Uncle Gil said. "Yep. He's my nephew. Tracker? Oh yes, the young man is obsessed with it and he's developed quite a bit of skill. Yes. Un huh. He mentioned that you might be calling, Sheriff. This is going to be out in deep country? How many with him?"

My uncle seemed to look concerned for a moment, then glanced at me. He could see I really wanted to do the job, this being the first chance I'd ever been offered to be paid as an actual tracker. Had I been a springer spaniel, I would have been jumping up and down and barking. He looked at Rosa for a moment then spoke into the phone.

"All right, Sheriff, he'll be there tomorrow, mid-morning, assuming we can agree on a fee." He said a figure that made my jaw drop and filled me with panic. They were never going to go for that amount, and I was sure to lose the job.

"Great, Sheriff Belshaw," Uncle Gil continued. "Mac and one our associates will be there. He'll find your man if he can be found. Thanks. Bye."

"They went for that?" I asked, astonished.

"Yep. You have a very specialized skill there, son. It's okay to charge a bit for it, 'specially since actual paying jobs of that sort are probably pretty rare." Uncle Gil paused a moment. "And of course, a third of the fee goes to your security." He looked at Rosa pointedly. Rosa looked at me, a question in her eyes.

It's taken me a while to learn to pause before I speak, but it's a habit that had saved me on occasion. Though I didn't think I needed 'security' on this, there really was only one acceptable answer to what was happening.

"Okay, then! I'll be glad to have Rosa backing me up. What can you tell us about the job?"

"Fugitive tracking in the Pasayten Wilderness." He related the rest of the conversation, probably hoping it would make me cautious. "Native guy, outdoorsman, wanted for murder. You just follow his trail. You're not in anyway to try and apprehend him. You're the tracker. Rosa, your only job is to watch Mac's back at all times."

"And I'm always happy to watch her backside all day long," I said. Uncle Gil rolled his eyes.

Rosa smacked me in the chest at the old joke, but she smiled. "Don't make me file for sexual harassment before the job even starts."

****

At 4:30 a.m. the next morning I pulled into the parking lot of our office, arriving a half hour ahead of schedule. Though my coffee hadn't by any means kicked in, I was there a half hour early on purpose. For once, as God is my witness, I was going to get to one of these early-rising rendezvous first.

Rosa's RAV was already there and she was sitting, listening to tunes and sipping coffee. As she exited her little Toyota, she smiled at me brightly, already quite awake.

"How… what… you're early!" I accused.

"Oh, Mac, you know I have you dialed in, don't you? You're so competitive!"

"And you're not?"

"Not the point." She was a half a step from laughing. "Let's go get *Nondescript* and get on the road."

Nondescript was a 1998 Acura that the company maintained for staking out neighborhoods where we wanted to remain unobtrusive. Painted black, it was old enough, that if it was allowed to get a little dirty, no one ever looked at it. It was the closest thing to invisibility that current technology and magic allowed. It was also one of those cars that never seemed to have mechanical problems.

Also, I wasn't the one who named it. Just sayin'…

We loaded our backpacks, secured our firearms, and we were off. Rosa wisely took the driver seat, the warp drive in my brain not yet active. She took us up the east side of the Columbia River, very little traffic to worry about other than early morning truckers pushing the speed limits. Somewhere around the bridge that takes the highway back to the west side of the river, the coffee set in and my brain finally kicked over. Conversation was now possible.

"Rosa, you think I'll do okay with this?"

"It speaks!"

"I'm serious, I don't want to screw up this job."

"What? You kidding? Last year you tracked that little girl in the pouring rain through a soaking wet forest. Fifty volunteers lost her trail, you found it within a half hour, and rescued her by the end of the day. Get real."

"Yeah, but I think this will be different. I was on my old home ground there, I've never even been up in the Pasayten Wilderness.

And from what little they told Uncle Gil, the guy I'm supposed to be tracking is a Native American dude, quite good in the mountains."

"And?"

"And he's probably good at counter tracking."

"Counter tracking? You mean like throwing you off the trail?"

"Yeah. He's gotta know that they're comin' for him. Maybe he's even booby trapped the area."

Rosa sat silently for a moment. "You think he might?"

"Ed taught me several man-traps he got from the Viet Cong. Said I'd probably never need 'em but thought I should know 'em. If this guy knows even a tenth of them, well… if I was him, I'd cover my bases."

"I'm not worried."

I looked at Rosa, a little astonished.

"I've seen you work in the outdoors. He won't catch you. And besides, you'll be going first, so I'm completely safe!"

"Rosa!"

"Don't worry. I promise to protect you from the bad guys."

"Now you're just being obnoxious."

The mood was a forced lightness, but it quickly deteriorated when the car was flooded with light from behind. I looked back and saw a huge eighteen wheeler hugging our rear bumper.

"Shit!" Rosa said, "Get off my ass, pendejo! I'm over my speed limit already, and you're supposed to go ten miles per hour slower!"

The driver had no intention of giving us a break, and when a wide shoulder came up, Rosa wisely pulled over to let him pass. The trucker gave two short honks of his horn in acknowledgement.

"Yeah," she muttered, "and the goat you rode in on."

"You want me to drive for a while?"

She looked down her nose at me. "I am quite capable of driving us."

"Didn't mean you weren't."

"I'm not the one who was tailgating. I'm the one who pulled over to get us out of dill weed's path."

"I never said…"

"So, if you don't mind, I will continue to drive."

"Works for me," I said, the picture of nonchalance. "I prefer sight-seeing anyway."

We pulled out again onto the highway.

"You have any idea how you're gonna start out?" she asked.

"If they can show me a first track, or a point last seen and just get out of the way, I'm pretty sure I can take it from there."

"Gil pulled me aside yesterday before I left for home. Told me to make sure they didn't send us out there unarmed. Police often don't like to have 'civilians' armed in their vicinity."

"I can't imagine they'd ask us to go on a flippin' manhunt unarmed!"

"We'll see. Since you're paying me to be your security, I just want you to know, we are not goin' out there with nothing but Swiss Army Knives."

"You don't want to see me in danger," I said, "and I sure as hell don't want to put you in danger. We're either armed, or we go home."

She took her eyes off the road for a moment, "Excellenté."

We came over a rise and down the other side, dropping towards the river again. Ahead, in the lightening darkness, we saw a couple sets of blue lights flashing on the side of the road. There, pulled over by not one, but two State Patrol cruisers was our trucker friend. The officers did not look too happy with him.

"It's a harsh world," Rosa observed, "and sometimes karma bites so quickly."

CHAPTER NINE

It was a long damn drive. Loman county was not exactly what you'd call centrally located, and its largest town, McClellan, was only about thirty-seven miles south of the Canadian border. Unlike its neighbors to the distant south, McClellan had done little to fancy up the town for tourists. It still had the old brick buildings, camouflaged under layers of chipping paint. Some looked like they had last been painted in the sixties, when the mining interests here began to dry up.

"Wow," I said, "I'm... whelmed."

"The scenery outside the town is nice though," Rosa replied. "You'd think they would have tried to capitalize on that a little."

"We're supposed to meet with Sheriff Belshaw at noon," I said. "and it's only 11:15. How about we stop there at Frankie's diner. My breakfast was two cold Pop Tarts eaten on the drive from my house to meet you."

"Mine wasn't much better, since I had to show you who the superior early riser was. Let's stop and eat."

"Hopefully, this isn't a super-slow service place," I said. We were lucky, the waitress, a blond lady in her fifties was efficient in that way only doing something for years on end can provide. Rosa and I both had hamburgers. It's undeniable, out of the way diners often have the best food, particularly when you're half-starved. I was pleased that I was able to buy lunch without having to count every penny.

"Where you two young folks from?" The waitress put our check on the table as she picked up dishes and cups.

"We drove up from Wenatchee. Here to see Sheriff Belshaw." Rosa gave me a raised eyebrow as I said it. Uncle Gil usually counsels us to keep our business to ourselves.

Our waitress's reaction was immediate. The friendly smile disappeared into a neutral mask and her body language went stiff. "I see. Gonna report somethin?"

"Ah, no. I'm here to see about a job doing some man-tracking for him."

"The Indian guy? Jim Three Feathers?" she blurted out, before biting her tongue. It was obvious she wished she hadn't said anything.

"Yep, how'd you know?" I asked, trying to hide the suspicion in my voice.

She looked down. "He was a regular. Seemed like a nice guy." She glanced at the man behind the counter who glared at her. "People can surprise you."

"Sometimes, it's the quiet ones," I said.

"Right." She leaned over as if picking up the dishes, whispering to us. "Be careful. Jim knows the old ways. That carries a lot of weight with the Okanogans and even the Colvilles – which could be dangerous for you."

"Thanks for the advice. People have been known to rally round an asshole just because he's one of their own," Rosa said softly.

She shrugged and walked behind the counter.

"That was interesting." I looked at my watch. "But we need to get going. It's quarter 'til." I plunked down cash and a tip and we were standing to leave when I realized the waitress was right behind me.

"If I were you," she said, looking into my face, "I'd be very discreet about mentioning what you're doing to anyone. I wouldn't want you kids to get hurt."

"Ah, thanks?" I said.

"We know almost nothing about him. He's a popular guy around here?" Rosa asked.

The woman shrugged again, and started to say something else, when a raspy voice interrupted her.

"Karen!" The unshaven man called from behind the counter. "Don't go wastin' these folk's time. You two got someplace you probably need to be, don'tcha?"

The invitation to leave was less than subtle. I nodded to Karen and we left.

****

We found the sheriff's office right at noon. I pulled the Acura into a side parking lot, avoiding the pines on the edges, which this late in the year loved to drop needles and cones over everything. The building was much newer than many of the places we'd seen in town, perhaps because it was funded by the county.

"I wonder what the property taxes are up here," I said as we climbed out of the car. "Be cool to have a cabin on twenty acres."

"This from the man who lives next to a wildlife refuge," Rosa said.

"Well, y'know. Grass is always greener."

We climbed the steps to the glass front doors and walked up to the receptionist. She was a native woman somewhere in middle age, heavy set and tired looking. She looked us over without expression.

"Can I help you?" she asked.

"Hi. My name's MacKenzie Crow. I have an appointment with Sheriff Belshaw."

Her gaze went flat. "Tracker."

"Uh, yeah, I am. Did you…"

She turned away from me and hit a button on her intercom. "Sheriff. There's two young people here to see you. Boy says he's a tracker."

Boy?

"All right. I'll send them back." She looked at us with all of the warmth of an early frost. "Down that hallway. Second door on the right."

"Okay, thanks."

As we walked down a hall through the building's center, I whispered, "Wow. That stick's is so far up her ass, it'll probably never see daylight again."

"Maybe, but that looked less like bein' uptight and more like quiet hostility. Remember what Karen at the diner said, Mac. Let's make sure we're always watchin' each other's back up here. Always." Rosa was dead serious. I didn't even think of making the usual joke.

"Yeah," I murmured. "It makes me think this Three Feathers guy has got some help out there. Maybe that's why they haven't caught him yet."

We came to a door, with *Sheriff* neatly lettered on the glass in a sedate serif font, and knocked.

"Come on in," a strong voice called out. We opened the door and Sheriff David Belshaw rose from behind his desk to shake our hands. He was around 5'9", with intense dark eyes, a round face that battled with heavy five-o'clock shadow and close-cropped dark hair, beginning to gray at the edges.

"I'm MacKenzie Crow, this is my associate, Rosa Fernandez."

"Sheriff," Rosa said.

"Pleased, I'm sure." Belshaw looked me over as we sat. "So, you're a tracker I hear. A pretty good one."

"I am," I said. This was no time for false modesty. "I've tracked for both the King and Chelan County sheriffs, though I'll tell you now it was SAR tracking. This is the card of the man I worked with in King County. He said he would be a reference for me, anytime."

He looked at the card King County Deputy Steve Dillon had given me, wrote down the number and handed it back. "I'll give him a call before we go out tomorrow. No offense."

"None taken. Lots of people say they're trackers, but don't practice half enough."

"Let me fill you in on what's going on here. About two weeks ago, one of my deputies responded to a call, shots fired out at a trailer on Hatchet Road. When he arrived, he found one Janice Lynde, dead from a gunshot to the back of the head, execution style. Her hands were tied behind her and her ankles were tied together. Evidence indicates she was kneeling on the floor when she was killed."

I couldn't help the distaste that must have shown on my face. Rosa's face was stoically neutral.

"This county has its problems. The people hereabouts live out here or moved here because they wanted independence from Big Brother. Unfortunately, some of these independent souls think that's means they have license to do whatever they want, including breaking the law," he said. "One of those independent things some few do, that I find most distasteful, is making meth in out of the way locations."

"And this lady was somehow tied to that?" I asked.

"We're pretty sure she was. There's evidence that Mr. Three Feathers and Ms. Lynde were involved in that very thing, according to a journal we found on her table. Her last entry mentioned meeting with Three Feathers only an hour before the call we received."

"That's pretty convenient, leaving evidence right by the body," Rosa said.

"We work with the evidence we have," a deep voice behind us boomed out.

Rosa and I both turned in our chairs to view a very large man in a deputies uniform. He was in his forties, big, muscular and with a hawklike face. The intimidation factor mellowed when he gave us each a warm smile and stepped forward to shake our hands. You start to learn to identify jerks of the male persuasion when they try to crush your hand with each hand shake. Though obviously a strong man, The man's handshake was cordial and wasn't an instant testosterone contest. I began to like him almost immediately.

"This is Deputy Cleeve." Belshaw gestured in the man's direction. "Cleeve, this is our tracker, Mac Crow. The young lady is Ms. Fernandez." Cleeve nodded at Rosa.

"Tracker, huh?" Cleeve said, "Sure hope you can do a better job than ol' Teeg, or this'll be a short man-hunt."

"There was another tracker on this?"

"Teeg's one of my... our deputies," Cleeve said. "He's pretty good at finding wounded deer in hunting season, so when we went to serve our warrant out at Three Feathers' cabin, he found the man's trail heading off into the wilderness. Unfortunately, he completely lost it about a quarter mile in."

I make a point of never dissing another tracker (mostly) so my question was carefully phrased. "Did he come to hard pan, or maybe rock?"

"Nope. Trail just up and disappeared."

That told me a lot. I nodded.

"Has it rained recently?" I asked.

"Nope, but I'll tell you I'm a little worried we might get some snow out there. We're overdue," Belshaw said.

"Sheriff, I'll have Holmes and Teeg ready to go first thing in the morning. Are you all set?" Cleeve asked.

"I'll finish up my pack tonight."

"Good. We'll all be here at first light. I'd recommend taking the M-16. I think Teeg's gonna need to carry the M-4. He's not a big guy."

"That works for me. Are you off now?"

"Yep. Headin' home. Gonna leave it in your and ol' Lincoln's hands."

"See you then."

Cleeve left and Rosa asked, "My... deputies?"

"You don't miss much, do you, young lady? Cleeve there, was the sheriff of this county until about two years ago. He... well, let's just say he wasn't real popular. When I moved here from Tacoma, I'd been a division chief there, and decided to run against him. I won with very little effort on my part." He sighed. "I rehired him because quite frankly, I needed someone with actual law enforcement experience. Cleeve, Holmes, and Teeg Mason have experience and were here before, but the rest of my staff, this is their first LEO job. Finding qualified people out here on the ass end of nowhere isn't easy."

"I see," I said. I had ton of questions about that, but discretion made me keep them to myself. It was going to be interesting going out in the bush with these men. They seemed qualified to have my back – and they certainly had the weaponry. Five of us against one man seemed like pretty good odds. I caught Rosa's eyes and stood.

"So, I assume you want us here at first light then?" I asked.

"That will be good. It's a long drive just to get to the cabin on some pretty god-awful roads. There's a motel just down the road called the Daylighter. Give them this card, and the department will comp your room. You two have your own gear?"

"We do. Both Rosa and I are experienced in the backwoods, and we work for a fugitive retrieval service. We have everything we need."

"That's fine. Remember that my people will be the ones making the arrest. Your service as a tracker will be much appreciated, but leave the fugitive retrieval to us. See you both tomorrow morning."

CHAPTER TEN

The Daylighter wasn't hard to find. It was one of those cheap motels you'll find on the edges of most towns, the ones where truckers might stay if they couldn't stand the sleeper cab one more night. Being as we were quite literally in the north woods, the walls were done in dark, somewhat depressing wood laminate. The bright orange carpeting, looked like a store remainder from the seventies.

"'Bout what I expected for free lodgings," I said to Rosa.

"I note we were authorized a single room with one queen-size bed," She said dryly.

"Um... bonus?"

"If you call you sleeping on that dinky loveseat a bonus, it is."

"Aw!"

"Aw!" she laughed as she mimicked me. "Sorry, boy, them's the rules."

"Seems to me that the person who's five-foot-seven should sleep on the dinky couch."

"Ai! Chivalry truly IS dead."

We unloaded the car and dropped our gear just inside the doorway. We also brought in the case with our M-4 carbines and the Glocks we both carried. No one wants stolen weapons floating around.

I was sorting through my old medium surplus ALICE pack when Rosa looked at it and I saw the all-knowing eyebrow go up.

"What happened to that nice Kelty pack your mom gave you for your birthday, Mac?" She said, "Why are you carrying that old Viet Nam pistol belt and rucksack? I see more repair stitches on that ruck than you'd see on Frankenstein's monster!"

I smiled. "I... kinda returned the Kelty, and exchanged it for a new down sleeping quilt. I paid a little extra and got one of those one pound jobbies. Most expensive piece of kit I've ever bought."

"Your mom must've been thrilled by that."

"I explained to her that this old pack and belt have a lot of sentimental value to me."

Rosa's eyebrow raised. "Sentimental value?"

"Didn't I ever tell you? This is Ed's ruck and belt. This is the gear he carried all those years ago when he was a LRRP in the army. The only thing new on this are the canteens. And some stitches."

"Ed was a long-range recon guy? I need to talk to that old man more. I had no idea."

"Yep. He gave me this stuff when I was seventeen years old, and I've carried it ever since then. For this trip, I took it off it's metal frame and I'm using the butt pack on the belt to hold it up a little. Most of what's in the pack will be my sleeping stuff, a few kit items and a jacket. Almost everything else is on the belt. It works good!"

"I'm not sure that using something this beat-looking is a good idea on a paying job, but I'm not the tracker. You're forgetting one thing though, you have to carry your vest and ammo for the carbine in there."

She was right. I had forgotten that.

"Okay, that's maybe another eight, nine pounds?" I said, "I can do nine more pounds. I just have to divvy more of my food to the belt and make sure the vest is in the map pocket against my back. It'll be okay, I've kept everything else light. Yeah. It'll be fine."

"You sound so confident."

"I'm sure it'll be fine, Rosa."

"Betcha five bucks the cops give you crap about your ratty gear tomorrow."

I was being rail-roaded and I knew it, but pride ever goeth before a fall. "You're on."

****

We had repacked everything, and rigged slings for our rifles when I realized the doomsday machine that is my stomach was once again crying for food. We had food in our packs, but nothing we wanted to eat while still in civilization.

"I think our reception at that diner might not be too great," I said.

"But I saw a burger stand on the way into town. Whatcha think?"

"I think I could eat. Let's go."

The burger stand was only a half mile back up the road, and Rosa and I had already spent too much time sitting in the car. We locked up our room and walked alongside the sparse traffic on the highway making it to the "Burger-Rama" in under ten minutes. We sat at one of the outdoor picnic tables and sparrows kept zooming in, trying to get a french fry.

"Good for a fast food place," I noted. "Nice view of the mountains through the pines."

"So, what'd you think of our clients?"

"The sheriff? Sounds like a lot of internal politics that I'd be thrilled to have nothing to do with."

"Yeah." Rosa looked thoughtfully at a small finch trying to get close to her french fry basket. "I sensed a lot of stuff there, undercurrents of office politics, but you know what the thing is that disturbs me?"

"The journal?"

"Yeah," she said. "You ever hear of a dealer writing down their partners names in a journal?"

"In movies, I guess. It'd be pretty damn stupid in real life."

"If you think that's stupid, would you write down who you're meeting with? Without using some kind of code? Even movies aren't that blatant."

"Ah," I said, "but you're forgetting that one word that takes some of the rough edges off - drugs. People on meth tend to send their IQ's southward at a tremendous rate."

"Assuming they're users as well as dealers."

"Happens that way a lot."

"People on Meth don't tend to write long journal entries either."

I thought about that a bit. I turned back to her and said, "We're here to track someone a law enforcement agency has an arrest warrant out for. That's the only dog we have in this fight. We have PI licenses, but that's only for legal purposes. Let's not borrow trouble."

Everyone on our team had taken the courses and been issued state private eye licenses. It gave us a bit more leeway in what we could and could not legally do in our pursuit of various fugitives. I was pretty sure my uncle had never intended that we use them to become freelance Sam Spades.

"Sî," Rosa flicked the end of a fry to the pavement, initiating a battle between four little birds, "but here's my take on it. Something smells a little funny on this. I just want for you and me to keep this in mind, to watch our backs, and to keep our situational awareness of everyone around us turned up to high. As your security guard, consider this my advisement."

"No arguments here."

****

The walk back was chilly. The late September temperatures dropped pretty fast when the sun went down, and I hoped we wouldn't have snow out in the mountains. It was easier to track in, but not very pleasant if it got deep.

It felt good to stretch our legs, even though we'd soon be stretching them a lot if we were going to track Three Feathers back into the wilderness area. I was walking along, minding my own business, when I felt someone's hip bump me into the ditch and only with some acrobatic scrambling did I manage to not land in the running water there. Rosa took off running.

"You little…" I yelled, "I'll get you my pretty, and your little dog too!" The pursuit was on!

"White men can't run!" she tossed back over her shoulder.

"Show you!"

We wound up sprinting the remaining quarter of a mile to the Daylighter and stopped in the parking lot, laughing hard and trying to breath at the same time. Trying to catch your breath and laugh at the same time is not as easy as it sounds, but suddenly Rosa wasn't laughing any more. I looked over at her and she pointed with her chin toward something behind me.

I turned, and saw two very large Native American gentlemen walking towards us with purpose in their strides and a distinct lack of friendliness in their eyes. The 90s vintage Buick they emerged from had another occupant, but I was a little too preoccupied to take a close look.

Rosa and I had both carried our Glocks with us, concealed under our clothes, I saw her casually move her right hand near the back of her belt. Mine was in a hidden pocket on the multi-pocket vest I was wearing, but I hoped this wasn't going to escalate.

The two walked up to us, and we all stood there, each waiting for the others to say something. Both men were youngish. The one on my left had closely cropped hair and a round face that still had acne problems. His shoulders were roughly about as wide as a motor home. The other was almost as big, with long hair the color of a ravens wing. He was handsome enough to make it into Hollywood movies, and not just for Native American roles.

"You're the tracker," Handsome said to me. He didn't seem to have any doubt. I wondered if perhaps I had a strange magic "tracking glow" around me, until I got a good look at the woman sitting in the car. It was the receptionist from the sheriff's office. Ms. Icicle Eyes.

"Yep," I said, in as friendly a manner as I could muster. "And you are?"

"Don't matter who I am. That your car over there?"

"Maybe," I replied, with a bit less emphasis on being friendly, "who wants ta know?"

"Jim Three Feathers is one of ours. He didn't do this thing they say he did, and you shouldn't go after him. Go back home."

"He shouldn't have run off if he's so damn innocent." I did not like this guy's tone.

Pockmarks didn't like my tone either. I could see his fists clench, and I knew where this was going without even being psychic.

"We're gonna give you a chance to do somethin' smart, white boy," Handsome told me. "You're too young to spend the rest of your life crippled up, so you and your little girlie there just grab your gear out of your room, load it in that car and head home."

"What a generous offer," Rosa said flatly.

"Keep it shut, bitch," Pockmarks said. "Just do what you're told."

Knowing Rosa, I decided that I'd better redirect the heat to myself. I didn't want too much blood spilt.

"Hmmmm," I said. "Hang on a moment... nope. I'm sorry, the *Department of Go Screw Yourself* says that's a no go. Sorry, fellas."

Pockmarks was moving to my right and away from Handsome,

the better to be able to hit me from two directions. I barely heard the click as the holster snap on Rosa's hidden Glock was clicked off and I shifted to my right, mentally hoping we could keep this firearm free. I wanted to work in this county.

Handsome moved a little to my left and I heard gravel crunch as Pockmarks suddenly charged. He was a huge man, with huge hands much like one of my karate sempai, Renaldo. Renaldo, a few ranks behind me had a tendency to charge in just that manner and I treated my attacker the same way I treated my dojo brother. I just did it a *lot* harder.

Pockmarks had maneuvered himself into, quite literally, one of the worst quadrants from which to attack me. The sidekick I sent his way hit him right in the solar plexus just as he was starting to breathe in. The impact was like kicking an oncoming train, but the effect was impressive.

He gasped explosively and landed on the asphalt hard on his knees. I whipped back towards Handsome, but he was of a more contemplative nature. He'd thought I was going to be intimidated enough so he wouldn't have to risk his pretty face.

He reached into his coat and produced a small fish billy club, the kind used to put a salmon out of its misery and tentatively started toward me. Rosa's Glock came out.

"Nope," I said, raising a finger in his face. "If you want your friend there to not suffocate, we need to get his solar plexus to end its spasm. I will need your help to do this. Put down the club, and you and I will help this guy to breath again.

He hesitated for a moment, not sure how to deal with the new situation, and I barked, "DO IT, NOW!"

He glanced over at Pockmarks, whose face was starting to get a blueish tinge and at Rosa's now visible Glock. He dropped the club.

"All right, man. Just help him!" he said.

"Get him in a sitting position," I said, "Good, now stick your knee in his back. Yeah, like that."

"How's this help?" he asked angrily.

"Grab both shoulders. Yep. Now, push forward with your knee, and pull back on his shoulders. Bend him backwards. Good, release it, and now do it again."

Pockmarks took a wheezy breath in and I had Handsome repeat the process a couple more times. Soon, though he wasn't breathing easy, Pockmarks was at least breathing. Handsome started to smile, but remembered he was in the process of running me off and frowned menacingly.

All of us jumped about a foot at the noise of the brief siren from the patrol car that had come up behind us. I was glad to see a representative of my current employers, until I saw the officer that stepped out of the cruiser was also Native American.

And I was the out-of-town white guy.

Rosa carefully placed her Glock on the asphalt and backed away, and the officer walked over, jacked out the magazine and cleared the chamber. He set the weapon on the cruiser's hood and walked over to our assailants. I noticed Handsome take several steps away from the fish billy as if to establish deniability.

"Ronnie. Mike. Mind if I ask what the fuck's going on here?"

"Officer," I interrupted, "I'm also carrying. We have CC permits in our papers if you want to see them."

He looked at me a moment and nodded. "Please put your weapon on the hood with the other one."

I very slowly unzipped the Glock's pocket and removed my .45 using thumb and forefinger to pull it out. I set it on the hood while he watched intently, and then stepped back to Rosa.

"Thank you. Now, if someone could answer my original question?"

"These two guys took offense to our being here," Rosa said. "Evidently, someone got them wound up and sicced them on us." She pointed toward the car.

He looked at the Buick and his face went stony. "All of you stay right where you are. Do not flippin' move from the spots you are currently standing in. Understood?"

We all nodded except Pockmark who still hadn't made it to his feet. The officer walked to the car and motioned for the woman to roll down the window. When she did, we could hear them talking but couldn't make out the words, but as the conversation progressed, his words became easy to hear. His volume went up along with his anger level.

"Goddamn it, Nadine! This will probably be the end of your job at the department. What the hell were you thinking?" His face was getting flushed. The woman went quiet and looked down at the floor. After a few minutes, he came back over, looked at the two men who'd accosted us and jerked his thumb back in her direction.

"You two get out of my sight."

"What?" Rosa started, heat in her voice, "You're not letting them go? They attacked us…"

"Do you two want to press charges?" the officer asked, watching the Buick pull out of the parking lot.

"Yes!" Rosa said.

"Never mind, Rosa," I said. I was pretty shaken up that the lawman had just let them go, but that told me how it would go. We didn't have a bat's chance in hell of winning this fight.

She gave me an angry look.

"It's just our word against theirs. I think it would be better not to stir the pot. We have enough on our plates." I muttered under my breath, "It's not right, but we can't win this one, Rosa."

I could see she didn't like it, but she nodded.

"You're the tracker, the one that the sheriff's gonna use to find my cousin, that right?"

Aw crap.

"I've been hired to find Mr. Three Feathers."

"Hmmmm," he said, contemplating the pavement. "Pick up your firearms, and lets go have a discussion. In your room there, if you don't mind."

CHAPTER ELEVEN

His name was Lincoln Davies. I didn't ask why his name wasn't more like the man we were hunting, Three Feathers. It wasn't my place, and he didn't seem inclined to share on the subject.

"Thanks for not pressing charges on those idiots. I'd see it as a real favor if you could just forget you saw Nadine in that car too. Good payin' jobs are hard to come by around here, and the sheriff's department pays a decent wage and some good benefits."

"Well," Rosa said, acidly, "she only tried to have us pounded into the asphalt out there, possibly crippled for life."

"And knowing my associate's marksmanship, things could have gone a lot worse for Mike and Ronnie," I noted.

"No one's arguing that. Though it's probably better for you as well that no one got shot," he said. "You have to understand that feelings are running pretty high around here, right now. A lot of First Nations people don't want Jim hunted, think it's some kinda vendetta from the sheriff. I work for the man, and I can tell you, Sheriff Belshaw's not like that. He doesn't like the whole thing anymore than most of my people."

"Mr. Three Feathers actually sounds like he has a lot of supporters. We've pretty much run into a wall of quiet hostility since we got here," Rosa told him.

"Jim is my older cousin. He lives way out there, but he spends a lot of time at our local tribal center teaching woodcraft, hunting skills, tracking… you name it, to the young ones. He's taken a real interest in making sure some of the things that his grandfather, Grady Three Feathers taught him aren't lost. I wish more of my people were involved in that."

Davies wasn't making this easier on me. The sort of things Three Feathers was doing was the sort of things that I really respected the most.

Shit.

"The evidence against him seemed pretty damning," I told him.

"Yeah." Davies looked down at his hands. "It's really upset a lot of people, and most of my people simply won't entertain the notion that the evidence isn't trumped up, a frame-up. I've known my cousin a long time, and though he had some brushes with the law when he was young and angry, I've found it hard to believe he would murder that woman, much less be making meth, but I'm the law, and he shouldn't have run. "

"Rosa here has a problem with how convenient that journal and meeting evidence was found."

"Jim's a tracker himself. He knows about obscuring a trail and he'd have to be stoned to be that careless," he agreed. "Nonetheless, he's got a warrant out for him. If this was the old department, I'd be all over the planted evidence notion if sheriff Belshaw wasn't in charge, but he's a real straight arrow. Used to be, the department's roster was lily white, but Belshaw's a good man, and if he says Jim has to be arrested, I'm ready to do it. Hell, there's so much money in drug smuggling these days, I guess anyone could be tempted."

I didn't know what to say, but Rosa always made up for that.

"We'll keep quiet about Nadine, if you'll tell *her* how close she got those guys of hers into serious trouble. You tell us about Three Feathers, so we're not goin' into this cold. The information we got from Belshaw wasn't exactly all that enlightening. What can we expect from this man, out there in the back of nowhere?"

For the first time, Davies smiled. "Mr. Crow, you better be one hell of a tracker, and even if you are, you got yer work cut out for you. I guarantee it. I can't imagine trying to find him without a lot of support at my back."

CHAPTER TWELVE

Rosa and I arrived at the sheriff's department parking lot at 5:30 a.m. We were the first ones there, by quite a bit, and we sat and drank our coffee and watched the sun rise over the forest to the east. At around 6:00 a.m., a Forest Service SUV pulled in, and one of their enforcement officers stepped out and stretched. I left the car and walked over to him.

"Hello. My name's Mac Crow. Are you with the group trying to find Mr. Three Feathers?"

"I s'pose I am," he said. "And you, are you with the team?"

He was very lean, athletic with red hair and freckles. His uniform was pressed and he carried what looked to be a .9mm pistol at his side.

"I'm here to track Mr. Three Feathers."

He seemed to relax at that. "Nice to meet you, Mac. I'm Bill Farnsworth. I'm here to represent the Feds since it's likely this will wind up in the wilderness area. Anyone else here yet? I was afraid I was going to be late."

"Nope. This is where we were told to meet up, but we've been here since five-thirty, and nada."

Rosa walked up, hugging herself to ward off the morning chill. "Hello, I'm Rosa Fernandez," she told him.

"And are you a tracker also, Ms. Fernandez?"

"Nope," she deadpanned, "bodyguard." And flicked her chin in my direction.

Farnsworth looked at me, a slight grin on his face. "Well. Good to know."

"Wouldn't want anyone else watching my back," I said.

We didn't have much of a chance to continue the conversation, a sheriff department SUV, a huge Suburban, pulled up and Cleeve and two other deputies stepped out. One of them, a smallish man with wispy blond hair, walked over and introduced himself.

"Hey. I'm Teeg Mason. That's Cleeve, and that's Holmes," he said, pointing to a quiet and efficient man unloading the vehicle. Holmes was roughly 6'3", around 250 pounds, had short blond hair, and looked like he'd given up his football career to come work in the outskirts of civilization.

All and all, I was pretty grateful for the brawn given the circumstances. My confidence in my backup was increasing.

"Who's the tracker here?" Teeg asked

"I am," I said. "Mac Crow. This is Rosa, this is Bill. Nice to meet you. Any idea when we're goin' to head out?"

"When the current sheriff gets his butt outta bed," a deep voice boomed. Cleeve walked up and nodded coolly to Farnsworth. "Feds, huh?"

"Federal wilderness," Farnsworth replied. "I'm just along for oversight. Won't get in your way, but I can help if needed."

Cleeve looked at him a moment, then nodded. "Hell of a safari to hunt one man, ain't it?"

Farnsworth started to reply when an older model Lexus sedan drove up and Sheriff Belshaw stepped out, still eating the last of his breakfast. He strode purposefully toward us, nodded to Rosa and me, and addressed Farnsworth.

"Bill, glad you could come with us."

"Glad to help out, Dave. Shall we get this show on the road?"

"Yeah. Cleeve, you and the trackers ride with Bill here. I'll drive our 'Burban' and Mason and Holmes can ride with me."

"Actually, Sheriff, I've been to his cabin before and you ain't. I'd suggest that I drive, you ride with the Fed, and you both follow us," Cleeve replied. "Save us time from gettin' lost."

I could see Belshaw wasn't pleased with the idea, but he acquiesced. "Fine. Just don't take off Hell for Leather and leave us behind. You and your high school cronies sometimes forget who's in charge."

"We never forget that, Sheriff," Cleeve said.

"Then let's get loaded and get this show on the road," Belshaw told him.

Rosa and I walked back to the Honda and got our packs. When we pulled out the carbines though, Cleeve walked over and stopped us.

"You civilians don't need to take weapons. There will be more'n enough security with all the officers around you."

Rosa looked over at me, the all-seeing eyebrow raised, and I nodded as covertly as I could.

"We're not going out there unarmed," she told him, "This is a man-hunt for someone suspected of murder and we're not going out completely defenseless."

"Completely unnecessary. We'll protect you."

"I'm sorry, unarmed is not an option." I kept my voice polite, but firm.

"What's the problem here?" Belshaw said, walking over to us.

"These two think they need to be armed on this little excursion."

Belshaw looked at us and grimaced. "We really don't need a bunch of extra firearms along on this. Just put 'em in your car, and let's go."

Rosa and I picked up our packs instead, and put them in our car.

"I'm sorry we couldn't do business, Sheriff."

Belshaw rubbed the bridge of his nose. "All right. Let's compromise. Leave the carbines in our gun locker here at the station, and you can take your side arms. Will that work for you?"

I looked over at Rosa, saw an almost imperceptible nod. We pulled our pack out of the car and followed Belshaw into the station to store our carbines.

"You cave too easy, Sheriff," I heard Cleeve say behind us.

"But I am the sheriff, and you're not," Belshaw said without looking back. "Please try to remember."

****

The roads got progressively worse. We left the pavement for a very well graded, graveled road that went on for miles, then turned off on a rougher road that had probably originally been for logging.

"So, Dave. Cleese," Farnsworth broke the silence of the SUV's cab, "trouble with the former sheriff?"

Rosa and I were sitting in the back seats, and from my position behind the driver's seat, I could see Belshaw's pained expression. "He and Holmes are both a pain in the ass. They haven't given me reason or proof to fire 'em without risking a lawsuit, but as more and more people move here to get away from it all, I'm seeing that these two local dinosaurs may have to go."

"Dominic Cleeve has been acting like local aristocracy since high school, and Holmes has been his right hand man since then," Farnsworth said watching the forest roll by outside his window. "He went right from captain of the football team to the army and we all hoped military service would have tempered some of the piss and vinegar out of the both of them. No such luck."

I looked at Rosa and she returned the look, eyebrow raised.

What the hell kinda turf war are we getting into here?

"We were so goddamned understaffed and those two had the experience a new sheriff needed," Belshaw said. "Hell, I'd only lived here two years before I decided to run against him. When I won, he came to me for a job, hat in hand, humble seeming. Now, the honeymoon's over, but we all have to work together. I want all these amateur 'Breaking Bad' tweekers out of my county, and for that, I need everyone I can put in a unit. Cleeve can drop the hammer hard when I direct him to."

"I've never liked Cleeve," Farnsworth said, "and I don't really trust the man."

"The federal government's track record on being right is a little wobbly from where I sit. Right now, I need Deputy Cleeve doing his job. The sheriff's department may have some problems, but they *will* be sorted eventually."

The rest of the ride was pretty quiet after that.

Miles later, we turned on a rutted side road that looked like the only maintenance performed on it were the occasional tire tracks going up its steep grade. With some straining by the government SUV, we managed to make it up the hill.

A little over two hours after we'd started, we were at Three Feathers' rustic cabin. When I say rustic, I mean most of the building materials had either come directly from the forest or from a junkyard. It was an amalgamation of lodgepole pine, mud chinking and rusty sheet metal. But it looked snug and the stove pipe coming out of the roof told me it was probably warm when it needed to be.

We pulled up next to Cleeve's vehicle, and everyone started to get out.

"Sheriff, can I get everyone to stay near their rigs for a few minutes? I'd really like to get a look at the area before everyone tromps across it," I said.

"All right. Be aware my deputies were here a few days ago."

While everyone else unloaded, I wandered the area around the cabin, carefully observing the ground and signs it held. There were several tracks around, and I was familiar with the tread pattern. I looked over at Cleeve, Holmes and Mason, they all had military style "desert" boots on, all in desert tan. Most of these prints must have been made five to seven days ago when they first tried to serve the warrant. Unfortunately, I hadn't been here long enough to know the recent weather for more than a day or two before. This made it more difficult to be very precise, but it was obviously true that they'd been out here.

I noted that both Farnsworth and Belshaw wore what looked like Timberland boots, and of course, Rosa had her Danners. I was wearing a somewhat worn pair of Columbia trail-runners that were supposed to be water proof. Supposed to be.

It was good to know the tracks of all the players before we set out.

I noted that I only saw the combat boot tracks. Nosing around, I saw the deputies' tracks went up on the small porch. I was surprised to see a faint track leading to the door. In fact, it was the back half of a footprint and it was bisected by the door.

The tracks didn't lie, one of the officers had been in the house. I glanced at the door handle lock and saw tiny scratches around it. I wondered what that was all about. Had they had a search warrant, or hadn't they? It looked like someone had picked the lock.

I also found a set of large footprints that looked several days older than the others. They had very worn tread. I could see that even with a week of erosion in the tracks. At the side of the house, I found the same tracks, much more deeply indented heading for a faint trail leading up the hill. The combat boots also went on this trail and in many cases stepped on the older tracks.

"When you're tracking you don't step on the trail you're following!" I shook my head. I walked back to the SUV to get my gear.

Rosa was testing out her lightweight Osprey pack, and tightening straps here and there. After a little trip with me last year, we had started to get into a competition about who could have the lightest pack and she was beating me by buying ultra-light camping gear. I was barely keeping up, usually by leaving stuff at home, but this time, I was carrying everything I might need.

Rosa saw something I hadn't left at home as I strapped it to the back of my leather belt and hid it under the pistol belt butt pack and canteens.

"Mac," she whispered. "You brought the Cutlass? Seriously? This isn't one of your survival treks. These guys are gonna seriously wonder about you if you're carrying a big-ass knife!" But there was a smile on her lips.

"Can you see it under the canteens?"

"No, but if you have to hide it during this fiasco, why take it?"

"Rosa, this knife has saved my life twice. I just feel... I dunno... naked without it now."

"Ancient religions and big knives won't beat a good blaster at your side," she said, reaching behind her and patting her .9mm Glock. "Make sure your gun is on your belt too."

I smiled at the reference and put my holster on the old pistol belt.

"What the heck kinda pack is that on your back?" Cleeve said, as we all moved to a central spot. I sighed, and without answering him, handed Rosa her five bucks.

She laughed.

CHAPTER THIRTEEN

After a brief but un-needed pep talk from Belshaw, we all started up the trail behind the cabin, with myself in the lead. With the tracks of the deputies over laying his prints, I almost didn't have to see Three Feathers' tracks. The men who had followed him the first time were much less attuned to the outdoors and left an obvious trail. I could see our quarry's tracks, but they were much more faded, even though the depth of some of them told me he was wearing a backpack when he headed for the hills.

I stopped for a moment, and Teeg Mason trudged up to me, burdened under his own pack, obviously too heavy for him. "This guy's tricky," he said to me. "I don't know where the hell his trail went, but it was like aliens came down and took him from above."

"We'll find him."

"Yeah, I hope so too. We gotta catch this dude." He paused for a moment, "Um, look man, I just want you to know… I'm.. Sorry we got you into this."

"Sorry?" I asked, "Don't be sorry! I get a chance to prove my skills against someone who really knows what they're doing out there, *and* I get paid for it. This is like heaven!"

"Yeah," he said with a sickly grin, "Heaven." He turned and trudged back to where Cleeve and Holmes sat by themselves.

"I wonder what the heck that was about," Rosa said, watching him go.

"I'm guessing that our local deputies there are a lot less confident about being able to bring Three Feathers in than they let on. We'll be on his turf, he's really skilled, and he's willing to kill."

"Yeah. Maybe. Just remember though, Mac, we're the bird dogs. Not our job to go after the guy, just to point him out, like bloodhounds."

"Yes, Dear."

"Don't stot wit' me, Gladys." Rosa's elegant Latina accent switched to classic Bronx.

I moved up the trail following the tracks until I came to what must've been the Point Last Seen, where Mason lost him last time.

"Teeg! This the spot?"

"Yeah. This is it. He just disappeared."

He was right. I could see where the other deputies had waited, a couple cigarette butts telling me they had sat and smoked while Mason tried to find the trail. Teeg's tracks went out, came back, went out another direction, came back, went out once more. I was guessing, but the track on one of his return trails was deeper than the other two, heels hitting harder and I was pretty sure he had been almost stomping coming back. Maybe angry, maybe embarrassed.

But he'd been right, the trail had literally disappeared.

When you lose a trail like this, you have to look at the landscape. The landscape will dictate what's possible, and how the trail will play out. The last track of Three feathers ended where his trail went by the base of a rocky cliff, and close inspection of that last track showed a pushout, where dirt had mounded up from pressure on the entire left side of the track. That indicated that he had moved to his right, forcefully, but that made no sense.

"Trouble?" Rosa had seen the furrows in my brow, I guess.

"I can see why Teeg was stumped. He kept going out ahead, hoping to find more tracks, but I think maybe this guy climbed the cliff, but the tree's in the way and there's no sign here that he climbed the tree."

It made no damn sense.

Rosa looked at the limbs hanging down. "Maybe he's part ape?"

Something clicked. Limbs hanging down... I'd been looking at the trunk, thinking you'd have to grab with your feet to get up the tree. I noted how the limbs were situated and walked to the other side of the tree. As I studied the ground, I saw a small piece of the wolf lichen that grows on Ponderosa pines lying on the pine needles.

Could've easily have been a squirrel. Maybe.

About ten feet up, bark had been knocked loose. Just a small piece.

"But he was wearing a frickin backpack..." I dropped my ruck and started to climb the tree.

When I made it to the missing bark, I was high enough to see the limbs below and the slight damage to the tops of their bark. As I climbed farther, Belshaw came up, looking at me with a perplexed expression.

"Oh come on, you're not telling me..." he started.

"Just let him do his thing," Rosa said, hand raised.

I started climbing again, and I noticed there was an overhang on the cliff face, one that actually jutted out towards the tree. I kept climbing. I went up to about ten feet above the overhang where it had formed a ledge, with the entire cliff face going back at a less steep angle.

"Oh hell, yeah." The picture became clear. There was a large patch of moss on the ledge, and even from the ten feet away I could see it had been replaced. He'd torn it loose, jumping with a full backpack across the intervening five feet from the tree. My respect for Three Feathers' skill and hutzpah went up dramatically.

"Got something," I called down. All of them had clustered around the tree to watch me do my monkey imitation.

"Whadya see up there, son?" Cleeve called up.

"I found traces he climbed up here and jumped to the ledge over there. Gonna see if I can follow."

"Oh Christ! Don't!" Belshaw exclaimed, but I was already jumping.

It was close. I landed on the ledge with both feet, wavered, then threw myself forward and grabbed the rock. I was there. And I could see a path off the rock face. Dropping down low, I could see indentations in the moss. Faint footprints.

Gotchaaaaaa.

I carefully moved off the ledge and worked my way across the more level section. There was only one way off the rocks without technical climbing, and as I suspected, the faint outline of a track awaited me where stone again met dirt. He had stepped onto pine needles, but I was sure at this point he wasn't worried about anyone finding how he had disappeared. Though faint, the tracks led through the trees and over the hill.

"Did you find him?" Rosa asked as I came down the steep hill.

"Found his trail. Sorry to tell you all, but we're leaving the flat. He went up the hill here," I said as I picked up my rucksack.

"Oh great," Teeg said. "Just great." They all hefted their backpacks and we continued the hunt.

****

The rest of the day was slow going. I began to believe that Three Feathers was the kind of man who was careful as a matter of course. There were no more obvious attempts at counter tracking, but even with the heavy pack on his back he was a man who moved leaving little trace.

He might have been a drug dealer, but he didn't take drugs. He was too tuned in. And too skilled.

I managed to keep on his trail for a good twelve miles, but the intense concentration needed was taking its toll. At around 6 p.m., I lost the track yet again, and I was pretty damn glad when Belshaw called a halt.

"That's enough, Mr. Crow." We're losing the light here, and we have no idea how far we'll have to go in this pursuit. Let's stop near this creek and make camp."

Rosa and I were going to sleep under a tarp and I was a little surprised to see the sheriff and his deputies erect three separate dome tents and start loading their sleeping gear inside. No wonder their packs looked so bulky.

Rosa was organizing our light pads and sleeping gear. I noticed she had put our bags end to end, so that my head was at her feet.

"Sure you don't want to zip our bags together, y'know, for extra warmth?" I oh-so-casually asked.

"Down, Wolf Boy," she said, grinning. "We *are* hardened professionals here."

"A guy can try," I said, sighing. "Did you see all the stuff they pulled out of those huge packs? No wonder I kept getting out ahead of everybody."

"Farnsworth has a tarp, just like us, and a small pack. Notice though, he stayed back with the other law boys. Like he didn't want to let them out of his sight."

"Feds and local law. Sometimes, not a lot of trust between them, and Farnsworth is kinda responsible for this area."

"Maybe. Did you notice the weapons Cleeve and Holmes are carrying?"

"Tell me," I said. I had been pretty obsessive about the track, and when I'm tracking, I can get a bad case of tunnel vision.

"Cleeve is carrying an old deer rifle with a scope, and Holmes has an ancient looking twelve gauge strapped to the side of his pack. They have a lot of their gear out of their packs, but I note those packs are still standing up, leaning against a tree, and looking far from empty."

"What are you saying?"

"Seems like an odd choice of guns. I wonder if there are more modern weapons in those packs," she said.

"Maybe they want to make sure all of their armament bases are covered?"

"Maybe." She said, looking at me with eyebrow raised. "If I was them, I'd sure have newer, more tactical weapons though."

"Maybe they have a small budget."

"Maybe. But they are a law enforcement agency. You'd think modern weapons would be a priority. I wonder what our fugitive, Three Feathers, is packing?"

"Probably the same sort of hunting weapons. Of course, these days you never know what kind of arsenal these dudes livin' in the woods might have."

Since I had joined our bounty hunting firm, I had seen fugitives produce everything from a reproduction Colt Navy black powder pistol to a fifty caliber sniper rifle. Fortunately, most of them had been wise enough not to aim them at us. They didn't want to get shot, and we didn't want to shoot them. Having a fancy gun is not the same as being ready to use it on another human being.

"How are you two getting along?" Farnsworth walked up to our camp and sat on the ground, leaning against a tall pine. "I have to admit, I'm a little sore in the legs."

"My eyes are a bit bleary," I told him. "Staring at the ground for hours on end can start to wear on you."

"I suppose it would. Do you to mind if I sit with you to cook dinner?"

"The air pretty chilly over there by the deputies?"

"Ah, you noticed."

"We're about to get out our stoves. What's goin' on?" Rosa asked.

"Being a fed, I usually get a little distancing from the locals, but these boys are a case unto themselves. Belshaw's reasonably friendly, but the deputies simply look at me when I try to strike up a conversation. Or they'll reply with one word sentences if they absolutely have to. Doesn't hurt my feelings, as their reputation precedes them, but they're not being easy to work with."

"Reputation?" Rosa said, pointedly.

"I don't want to talk down fellow officers," Farnsworth said.

"Mr. Farnsworth, I know you may not find this easy to believe, but I am here for security for him." Rosa jerked her thumb my way. "As well as havin' a personal stake in his wellbeing, I'm being paid to keep him safe as possible. If these guys are a security risk, I want to know about it. This isn't a happy backpacking trip. We're hunting a man, one who knows the woods, and I'm not risking my client if the support is not there."

Her deadly seriousness took both Farnsworth and myself by surprise. I started to speak and she raised the "immutable forefinger of silence," also giving me the deadly look of "don't, just don't" and I went quiet. When men are confronted with this much female willpower, there is no defense.

"I..." Farnsworth hesitated. "Well, it's just that under Cleeve's watch as sheriff, there were a lot of complaints about... abuse of prisoners and missing evidence. Nothing was ever proven, and the complaints were usually later mysteriously withdrawn. But I think the county heaved a collective sigh of relief when Belshaw was elected. When he, in my opinion unwisely, hired Cleeve as a deputy, there was no small amount of astonishment."

"Can these men be trusted to do their jobs?" she asked. "That's my issue here."

Farnsworth looked toward Belshaw's men, "I'm pretty sure they can."

"Ah," Rosa said and dropped the matter.

I knew exactly what she was thinking. When someone says "I'm pretty sure" what they mean is "I'm not sure at all." I decided on a little personal research.

I rose and walked over to where Teeg Mason sat. "So, Teeg, I'm always interested to hear about other trackers and where they got their training. Who taught you, or did you learn on your own?"

He looked at me with a pained expression.

"Hey," I said, "I don't mean anything by it. I just wanted to get to know a fellow tracker a little better is all."

"Look, man," he said. "No offense, but let's just keep this all professional. I don't need to get to know you. You don't need to know about me. All we gotta do is find the injun. Let's leave it at that, okay?"

"Oh. Ahh… Okay, if that's how you think we should play this."

"That's how I think we should play it."

"All right." Awkwardly, I got to my feet and walked back to Bill and Rosa.

Rosa must have seen something in my face. "What is it, Mac?"

"I… that was weird. I just went and tried to talk to Teeg about where he learned, but he shut me down right away. Said he didn't need to know me, and to just keep things professional."

"Told you they were strange," Farnsworth said.

Rosa began to chuckle.

"What?" I said, slightly irritated at her reaction.

"Maybe he thought you were hitting on him!" she said. "He don't want none o' yer funny boy ways!"

"You know I'm not gay!"

"Oh yes, I DO know that. But a man of Deputy Mason's limited experience probably can't tell up from down in that department."

"Even if I was gay, I sure wouldn't be attracted to him."

"Your lips say no, but your eyes say yes!" Rosa laughed.

"What was it you said earlier? And the goat you rode in on!"

****

I was walking through the camp, taking our dishes over to the little stream to get water when Holmes, standing against a tree, called out to me.

"Hey. Tracker. You and the little lady gonna be sharin' a tarp hunh? Must be nice."

"It's not like that, man. Certainly not on a job."

He looked over at Rosa who was, unfortunately at that time, on all fours facing away from us, fluffing out our quilts. Holmes smiled like a wolf and it was all I could do to keep my face a mask and not punch him in the throat.

"Just sayin' if I was..." he started.

"Holmes," a deep voice said from behind us, "show some damn class." Cleeve stepped out of the darkness and jerked his thumb towards their part of camp.

"Didn't mean nuthin,' boss." He nodded to me and walked away.

"I'm sorry about that, Mr. Crow," the big man told me. "Holmes is a good man in many respects, but his attitude about women needs work. That young lady, I've seen how she moves, clean, careful, crisp. She's strong. Military?"

"Marines. She was an MP in Iraq."

"She looks tougher than some of the men I served with over there."

My surprise must have shown.

"I was in Desert Storm, then I was reactivated in '04. You shouldn't be surprised. The Army needed every man-jack they could get a uniform on for part of that war. I had an officer in our battalion that was fifty-eight freakin' years old. He could kick a lot of the younger guys' asses."

"I didn't mean to be surprised, it's just... what group were you in?" I asked.

"Rangers. You weren't in, were you?"

"Ah. No."

"Didn't think so. You have a certain innocence around the eyes still. Your girl there, young as she is, doesn't. I learned some hard lessons over there, some lessons that most folks definitely wouldn't agree with, but most folks have rose-colored glasses on." Cleeve's voice was momentarily bitter. "But let's not go into that. I was pretty impressed with the tracking you did. Damn impressed."

"Thanks."

"You must've put a lot of time in to learn that," he said. "I just want to warn you, we got pretty good at tracking insurgents over there, but they got really good at laying traps. This man we're tracking, Three Feathers, keep in mind that he's a crafty bastard too. Tracks are not the only thing you need to keep your eyes peeled for, you get my meaning?"

"Traps?"

"Yep. You know what the best way to keep from being tracked is?"

"Yes," I said. "Kill the tracker."

"Got it in one, son."

CHAPTER FOURTEEN

I was up before sunrise, and when Rosa saw me stuffing my gear in my belt and pack, she began to do the same. We probably shouldn't have bothered. We sat there for another hour, eating breakfast and watching the sun come up, until Farnsworth came over. Most of his gear was packed, but his tarp was still up. We all sat together in the morning chill, talking softly, waiting for the sheriff and his deputies to join us..

"I hope we can get this show on the road pretty soon," I said. "When the light is slanting like this, it really makes the tracks stand out."

"Well," Farnsworth said, "I think it's late enough, we should stop keeping our voices down."

"Maybe so," I said, a little more loudly than needed. "I think Rosa and I'll take a little walk ahead. Make sure I can pick up the trail again."

Rosa didn't look happy about leaving the group. "Are you sure that's a good idea, Mac?"

"I don't think we're near him yet, Rosa. But if we wait around, the sun's gonna be straight overhead when these guys get their butts in gear. That won't help me at all."

"You wanna come with us, Bill?" she asked.

"No, I think I'd like to stay here and keep an eye on the crew. Maybe I can convince them to get up and get moving. Just don't go too far out from us."

It really only took me about fifteen minutes to find Three Feathers' trail again. I'd been tired the night before and the light had been getting steadily worse. With this new morning, our quarry's tracks stood out to me, almost easy to see in the angled light.

"He's heading up the toward the end of the valley. I bet we're gonna end up in an entirely different drainage soon," I told Rosa.

"Did you see any indication that he camped?"

"No."

"Could it be he knows this area so well he just kept trampin' along in the dark? I mean, we're pretty much just going on game trails here." Rosa turned a 360, taking in the deep valley forest around us.

She was right. We hadn't come up the valley on the well-made trails most hikers were used to. Three Feathers had made sure, when he bugged out from his cabin, to take a route that few others would walk.

"Let me pull out the map to see if I can get an inkling where he might go." The USGS topo map that I had brought with me showed a good deal of country. It was one of the old, larger versions, and it took me a while to find where we had camped last night. "I wish we'd brought Farnsworth with us. If this area is his bailiwick, then he probably knows it pretty well."

"What? The Outdoorsman el Grandé needs someone's help?"

"Hmmmm," I said flatly, "why did I bring you, again?"

"I'm keeping you safe. So, sooooo safe." She smiled brightly as she said it.

"Hrrm. Well. I'm not on my home range here, and I'm fine following these tracks," I said, "but there's a lot about where we are now that I don't know. Look how close the Canadian border is. If Three Feathers slips across that, this hunt is over. Does he have another cabin out here somewhere? And if I was going to put a cabin out here, might I make some of the same choices that he might?"

"So much guesswork," Rosa said, shaking her head.

"Tracking is half science, half intuitive art." I said.

"Well, hopefully you can intuit our prey before he decides to switch countries."

"If there's a chance, we'll catch him," I told her.

And then, something was wrong.

My gut clenched and there was a tingle on the back of my neck. I started looking around and Rosa picked up on my change in mood.

"What is it, Mac?"

"I don't... know. I just got that... feeling. My gut says someone or something may be watching us."

Most people might have scoffed, but Rosa put one hand on the Glock at the back of her belt and with the other pointed at the crook of where some downed logs had fallen on each other.

"Let's take a break and sit here," she said. It was the best cover we could have found in the area we were in. We crouched down and scanned the woods. I'm pretty good in the woods, but I saw nothing I could point to that was out of order. No noise of branches cracking, no indication from the birds that anything was other than normal.

Maybe I was going crazy.

"Maybe I'm losing, it, Rosa," I said. "I got nuthin'. Just that weird feeling."

"Y' know what? I'll listen to your 'weird feelings' when we're out here long before I'd listen to the blustering of those slackers we came out with." Rosa rose up slightly and called out, "Who's out there?"

The forest around us was silent for a moment, then a man's voice came back. "Not Bad!"

"Mac! He doubled back on us!" Rosa was rummaging through her pack. "Get your vest on, right now!" I rushed to comply.

"Mr. Three Feathers?" I yelled.

"Jesus. They're sending babies after me now." The voice called out from what seemed like a different direction. "You trackin' me, young fella?"

"Yes. I am," I said, shrugging into my vest. "Any chance you could just make it easy on me and come to surrender?"

There was silence for a time, and then the voice once again came from another direction.

"You two, wearin' them bullet proof vests... if I was gonna kill you, them vests wouldn't be much help."

"You planning on killin' us then?" Rosa yelled.

"Ain't never killed no one. Hope not to, neither."

"Mr. Three Feathers, they say you killed a woman down there. What was her name, Rosa?"

"Janice Lynde."

Again, silence, then a different direction for the voice.

"I know who she was. Didn't kill 'er. Never even so much as spoke with the woman."

"The sheriff has evidence…" I started.

"I'm sure he does, and I bet I know who found that evidence too." The voice sounded bitter now. "You two listen to me. You give this up. Go back to where ever it is you came from, and track people who need help. I'm tellin' you now, this is only gonna end in tears. Go. Home."

"If you came back, I know Sheriff Belshaw would see you'd get a fair shake!" I yelled to the woods.

Silence.

"Mr. Three Feathers?"

Nothing. Just a few baseline birdcalls and wind in the quaking aspens.

"Mr. Three Feathers!"

"I think he's gone, Mac."

"Holy crap! He could'a jacked us big time."

"It makes me wonder one thing," Rosa said.

"What?"

"Is there anyone left in this county who hasn't told us to go home?"

****

"Have you found the trail?"

We had sat and waited for the others to join us, not really willing to move out of the logs we were sitting amongst. When Belshaw came casually sauntering out of the woods, I, for a moment, expected his chest to blossom with a high powered rifle round.

"He was here," Rosa told the sheriff. "He spoke to us from out there." She gestured toward the darker shadowed part of the woods.

"What!?"

"He spoke to us. We never saw him," I said. "He told us he didn't kill anyone. I don't know how he did it, but we could never quite tell where his voice was coming from."

"Don't matter what he said," Cleeve said, walking out of the trees.

"There's a warrant for his arrest, and he's fleeing." He raised his voice. "He's a damn fugitive, and we *are* going to take him back!"

I wondered if he was trying to convince Three Feathers or himself.

"Didja find the trail or not?" Holmes joined us. Mason and Farnsworth were close behind him, looking around nervously.

"Yeah, I did, but I think it would behoove us to have me cut for sign by circling this area and see if I can find a fresher trail. If he's gone, which I'm not sure he is, then he's left super-recent tracks and he can't be that far ahead."

Belshaw nodded, and I headed to where I thought the voice had come from last. I heard something behind me and looked over my shoulder. Rosa was there, and her Glock was out, in her hand and ready for action.

Once out of the meadow and in the trees again, I saw what a difficult time I'd let myself in for. If you've ever been out in deep forest, woods that are not tended by harvesting or regular visitors, you'd see that it's often a maze of blown down trees and brush.

"I can't believe he's playing the ninja game in all this," Rosa said.

I didn't say anything, my senses attuning to the shadowy world under the forest canopy. If what I thought I would find was actually here, it would make things a lot easier. It only took a minute or two to confirm what I was looking for.

"Look, can you see the game trail that parallels the meadow?" I asked.

"Do you mean that?" she said, pointing to a faint path.

"Yep. The deer always make trails about ten feet back from the forest edge at almost every clearing. They work the edges until they're reasonably sure it's okay to actually step out into the open and go where there's more food." I pointed where, if one looked, a very faint trail followed the outer contour of the meadow. "It's always the path of least resistance, the easy way."

"And you think Three Feathers used this 'path of least resistance' trail?"

"He's too much a part of this world to waste calories, to waste energy making a new trail." I started down the faint path, looking for any trace of the man. "He wouldn't be trying to impress us and be crawling over all these blow-downs. It takes forever to get through this crap."

"Kinda sounds like you're guessing a bit there…"

"You can't always be sure," I said, leaning down. "But it's really nice when you're right." I pointed to a patch of moss that carried the unmistakable shape of a partial boot heel.

"This is good! We'll be able to get to him that much sooner."

"Maybe." I looked out from under the trees, up the valley where it narrowed. It looked like there was only one way out in the direction his tracks were going. Probably, farther on, this trail would merge with the trail I was already following. But could I be that complacent?

"There's a good sized creek running down the valley, and the old trail Three Feathers' been loosely staying to, heads right up toward that pass up there. I bet he goes right back to it once he's away from us."

"Then we could just go up the valley and not have to climb over all these dead trees."

"If it were anyone else, I'd say that, but he's a tricky guy. I think I'm going to have to stay on this trail. Rosa, will you go the deputies and tell them to hold for a bit while I check this out?"

"Sure! If you go with me. I'm not leaving you here alone. All he has to do is injure you, and this little manhunt is Tango Ulysses," Rosa said.

"What?"

"It'll be finito. Dead in the water. So let's go back together. The less you argue, the faster we can get on his tail again."

This protectiveness was getting a little irritating. "Rosa, I do have my own weapon, right here on my belt. I'll be fine."

She just looked at me, saying nothing.

"I have good awareness. I have a gun. You don't need to hover."

She didn't budge, she just stood there waiting.

"Fine," I sighed. "Let's go together."

She smiled. Rosa likes to win.

****

It was not easy tracking.

Though I had in fact found his newer trail, I was starting to think Three Feathers might be part antelope. Rosa and I were both starting to get tired. Even though we were moving down the most unobstructed trail under the trees, we still had to probably climb over thirty downed trees every hour. With packs on, even ones under twenty pounds, it was starting to wear us down.

"You sure we're still on the trail?" Rosa asked, sweat dripping off her nose.

"Yeah," I said, pointing down.

"Hey! Even I can see that one. Guy must be confident you can't stay on his trail."

"Except that I've stayed with him all this time. Why would he think I've gone blind all of a sudden?" I said, feeling perplexed. "Unless he wants to be sure I can't lose this trail."

Rosa looked at me, eyebrows raised. "You think he's playin' us again?"

"I don't know what to think!" I said it more harshly than I meant.

"Maybe someone needs to eat a Snickers. When he's hungry he starts to look like that famous celebrity, Mr. Dick Head."

"Sorry. Let's sit and think a moment." I wiped sweat off my face with my bandana. "I guess I might need a break."

"It's one in the afternoon; you've been at this since 8:30 this morning. Let's sit and eat."

With a little food and a little rest, I was doing much better. Just giving my brain fifteen minutes to stop concentrating gave me what I needed to start again. The trail came out of the trees in another quarter mile, and I was not surprised to find that it merged with Three Feathers' original trail.

"Dammit! I should have listened to my intuition," I groused, "Here's where his original line of travel is. He's using the same trail now, and we just wasted a bunch of time."

"Doesn't it make his trail easier to follow? That's weird."

"Yeah," I said, looking at the tracks. I could hear the others not far behind us. They had been paralleling the trail I'd been following so we wouldn't get separated. "Let's bring the deputies to this point."

Ten minutes later, I was showing Teeg Mason where the two trails merged.

"Teeg," I told him, "I think we' have to be very careful now. He knows we're after him, and I'd guess he's going to probably turn tricky."

"Shit. Like he ain't tricky enough."

"Would you mind sticking with me, maybe give a second opinion if things don't make sense?"

"You sure?" For some reason, he wouldn't look directly at me, looking away or at the ground. "I can see you're a helluva lot better than I am."

"You did okay 'til he pulled that stunt. I'd feel better with two sets of eyes on the ground."

"All right. If you think so," he said. He still wouldn't look me in the eye.

We moved along the sizable creek, Rosa behind us. As we went along, Three Feathers seemed to disguise his tracks less and less until we came to a ford in the creek. His trail went right in and across the creek. I could plainly see a single boot mark in the mud.

What the hell?

"Sheriff, if you all wouldn't mind waiting, I think Teeg and I need to check this out. Something's fishy here."

"All right, Mr. Crow. I'm sure you'll figure it out." I was glad he was feeling confident about it. I wasn't so sure.

Mason and I waded the creek and saw Three Feathers tracks heading up the game trail. Teeg started after them, the easier tracking reigniting his enthusiasm. We wordlessly moved up trail, out of sight of the others, and I knew Rosa was keeping an eye on our surroundings.

"Shit, man. If he keeps runnin' careless like this, we're gonna be on his ass in no time!" Teeg called back over his shoulder.

He was about fifteen feet ahead and was coming to a medium-sized rock in the trail. I could see huckleberry brush lying in the trail just beyond it, leaves starting to wilt. He started to step over when something pinged in my mind.

"TEEG! Stop! FREEZE!"

Mason evidently was a man used to following orders. He stopped his foot in mid-air and looked back over his shoulder. "What? What is it?"

"Pull your foot back, and set it down behind you."

He slowly did so, and I moved up alongside him.

"What is it, Mac?" Rosa asked.

"That brush has been broken off and laid there. See how the leaves are dying." I looked close, and saw a length of paracord going off, tightly strung, to the right of the trail. It led to another small clump of brush, and carefully hidden there was a simple carved trap trigger and a very sharp, very dirty wooden stake.

"Holy shit!" Teeg said, visibly shaken.

"Yeah." I picked up a downed limb and stuck it in the first bush. I pulled out a loosely made noose that led to the trigger and one jerk of the limb set off the trap. Something on the other side of the tree yanked the limb dead on to the pointed stake and when I looked on the other side of a big spruce, a roughly forty pound rock hung from paracord over one of the branches.

"Nice," I said. "Nicely done."

"Nicely done! He was tryin' to kill us!" Teeg yelled.

"No. He was trying to wound," I told him. "An old Viet Nam vet once told me the idea on traps like these is to injure one person, then someone else would have to take care of that person. Two people taken out with one trap. And I think that's not the only trick he was playing."

"Damn, what else?" he asked, looking around as if Three Feathers were about to spring out from behind a tree.

"Look at the tracks we were following, No, I mean *really* look."

He kneeled over one of the tracks, studied it for a few moments then looked back at me, questioning.

"At the base of the heel, that tiny plume coming off the back of the track. That should be in the front of the track. He's walking backwards in his own track. That's why the heels are so deep."

Mason's look was as indignant as I felt. I wanted to yell out to Three Feathers. To challenge him for trying to punk me. But… best to be professional.

"Let's backtrack to the stream."

CHAPTER FIFTEEN

I found out pretty quickly how we'd been fooled. Our quarry had back-tracked to the creek and the rushing water had cleared away most traces of him. The water was moving fast and cold and I was having trouble moving in it, so I grabbed a limb for a walking stick to steady myself.

Then I noted I was not the first to do so.

His footprints had washed away, but the deeper points where his stick had landed were still there. A hundred yards upriver, I found where he'd emerged and saw the hidden draw where he's most likely exited the valley.

Rosa had been paralleling my path, fighting her way along the creek, carrying both our packs. When I sent Teeg back to get the others, she sat next to where I was pouring water out of my shoes.

"Those ought to be comfy, now," she said.

"Yeah. Waterproof doesn't help when you're over your ankles in water. They're all nylon, they'll dry out. I've got spare socks for the evening."

"So. A trap," she said.

"Non-lethal, meant to wound and delay. Teeg almost got nailed."

She looked back toward where the others were coming up to join us. "Wounding him wouldn't have been much of a loss. Having just spent some time with that group, I'm not terribly impressed with their professionalism."

"I guess we'll see them shine when we find Three Feathers. At least, I hope we will."

"That Holmes jackhole was leering at me, big time when I was getting our packs, like I was sitting around naked, waiting to give

him a lap dance. Cleeve told him to grow up. Belshaw was flipping'
oblivious to it," she said. "I kept quiet so as not to make trouble for
you on your first big job, but I was tempted to knee-cap Holmes."

"Rosa, you don't have to put up with shit on my account."

She smiled at me, and I felt that familiar flutter in my stomach. "I
can be cool for a while, as long as you promise to help me bury the
body later."

"Done and done!"

The others came thrashing through the brush, under their mostly
too heavy packs.

"Goddamn," Belshaw, said, red-faced and strained. "Did we have
to go through every alder hell in existence?"

"Sorry, Sheriff," I said, shrugging. "I guess Three Feathers just
isn't very considerate."

"Teeg here told us about the trap he almost blundered into,"
Cleeve said.

"Anyone would have hit it, Dom!" Teeg said, face turning red.

"Maybe." Cleeve didn't sound convinced. "But ol' Three Feathers
is gonna get his eventually."

Our fugitive had moved up a steep crack in the ridge that a small
stream meandered out of and I led the way, hot on his trail. The
tiny canyon it formed was almost invisible from the lower part of
the valley, and it began to form a series of rock terraces filled with
a super short alpine moss that made them look like isolated golf
greens. I could see the impressions of footprints slowly springing
back up, but still visible.

The late fall weather was starting to turn cold, and our elevation
gain wasn't helping. I finally grabbed my baggy fleece and slid it
on over my ballistic vest. Rosa pulled her puffy jacket over her own
as well. The deputies' packs were heavy enough however, that they
were sweating in the cold. Holmes actually had a trace of steam
rising from his back.

We rose to a small plateau, steep-sided downward on three sides
with a rise on the fourth side that went up the mountain. I was just
about to step out of the little grouping of spruces the trail went
through when something, some intuition, caused me to look up the
hill.

"Sheriff! Three quarters up on the hill in front of us!" I whispered.

I pointed and the group looked to see Three Feathers moving crossways on a steep slope about 150 yards in front of us.

"Sheriff, we got him, let's send these three," Cleeve said quietly, gesturing at Rosa, Bill, and myself, "back down to the trees. We don't need them, and they'll be out of our way."

"I won't ask them to participate in apprehending the man, Cleeve," Belshaw said, "but if he sees this many people after him, he might just give up."

"I really think we should get the civilians out of the picture, just in case this gets ugly."

Belshaw looked at his chief deputy, and I sensed from his body language that he was too irritated at Cleeve to accept advice from him.

"We might need the support. They stay," he said.

"So be it." Cleve stopped for a moment, turned toward us and shook his head in what looked like aggravation. He gave a look to Holmes and Teeg Mason, an odd look, but I had no idea what it meant. Both men glanced our way, faces neutral. Teeg's body language went very tense.

I guess I'd be tense, too, if I had to apprehend a dangerous felon and had people I didn't know tagging along.

"James Three Feathers!" Belshaw yelled up the slope. "Halt! We have a warrant for your arrest for the murder of Janice Lynde. Drop your gear and put your hands on your head!"

Three Feathers stopped and looked down at us as we moved onto the plateau below him. He was too far away to see his facial expression clearly, but his tone was one of contempt.

"Belshaw," his voice boomed down to us. "That's a load of shit."

Rosa and I stepped away from the deputies, dropping our packs and clearing the field of fire if a firefight broke out. Farnsworth moved next to us, dropping his pack also, and we all stood on the edge of the steep slope, watching the drama unfold.

"I'm not the one who's been screwing around makin' meth and gettin' rich off it," Three Feathers yelled.

"That's for a court to decide, Jim! You don't help your case by laying traps for pursuing law enforcement!"

"When the one framing you *is* law enforcement…" Three Feathers words ended abruptly as a shot rang out in front of us. The man fell limply into the huckleberry brush and disappeared from sight. We all looked at Cleeve in astonishment, as he jacked another round into the old bolt action rifle.

"Cleeve!" Sheriff Belshaw almost screamed the deputy's name. "What the Goddamned hell are you doing?"

"What I have to, Davey." Cleeve calmly turned the rifle toward his boss and pulled the trigger. Belshaw's head snapped back, and a red spray erupted from the back of it. He rag-dolled over backward and landed in a heap. An unmoving heap.

CHAPTER SIXTEEN

In the movies, time seems to stand still when events like these occur. In reality, things happen so fast that you don't have time to process them.

We all stood unmoving for a moment, staring in shock at what had just happened. The click-clack of a shotgun cocking brought me out of it and I realized Rosa was the only one who'd been thinking while we stared at the scene.

She had her Glock up, arms extended and fired off a round at Cleeve. Then the shotgun blast caught her in the chest.

I was already turning to go to Rosa as she fell back over the lip of the hill and started to tumble. As I turned, I saw Holmes jacking another round into the ancient twelve gauge and Teeg Mason drawing down on me with a very non-regulation hand cannon.

"I'm sorry!" I heard him scream, then the sound of the pistol was all I heard. If I hadn't been moving to reach Rosa, I would have taken the round in the forehead, just like Belshaw. Instead, I felt the 1,250 foot-per-second round zip just past my head. The wind from its passing was like a slap.

I was below the lip of the hill a second later, running after Rosa trying to get to her, to stop her roll down the hillside. I reached her as she tangled in huckleberry brush, and I was dreading seeing her bloody chest. When I got there though, she was conscious and coughing, her puffy jacket-front in shreds and a few small blood spots on her arms, but the ballistic vest underneath was pretty much intact.

"Get her up!" Farnsworth was coming down the hill, firing with a .9 mm back up the hillside. "For God's sake, get her up and run! They mean to kill us!"

We both reached down, lifted her by her arms and began half carrying, half dragging her towards the shelter of the trees. I heard a shot behind me, and dirt spattered a foot to my right. Mason had just tried again with the hand cannon. The shotgun went off too, but didn't get near us. If Cleeve got us in his sights with the scoped 30.06, we were in big trouble.

Twenty more feet and we were in amongst the firs, and I heard Cleeve's booming voice. "After them, goddamn you! If they get out, the whole plan is screwed!"

"Stop!" Rosa wheezed, "Stop. We gotta keep them from coming after us!" I felt her hand at the retention holster of my Glock 21 and she pulled it free. That holster was designed to keep another person from accessing your firearm.

But Rosa knows guns like I know tracks.

She moved behind a tree trunk, kneeled, and began teaching our pursuers that chasing us might not be in their best interests after all. I'm not bad on the range, but I'm not even in her league with a handgun. She managed to put rounds very near Holmes and Mason, neither of whom were Hollywood action heroes. It was quite a distance, and if she'd been at 100 percent, probably at least one would have been dead. Both men, seeing they had no cover, turned and ran back up the hill. There was a puff of smoke and the bark above her head exploded as the Cleeve's hunting rifle replied.

"Okay!" she yelled, "We can go!"

We headed down the side path running to reach the valley. At the bottom, we moved through the alders, knowing the deputies couldn't be far behind. As we approached where we'd originally crossed, I called a halt before we emerged from the brush. Rosa was bent over and breathing hard.

"Why are we stopping?" Farnsworth demanded.

"Can you make it?" I asked Rosa.

"Yes... just... hurts."

Farnsworth started toward the trail to the cars.

"Bill!" I said. "Not that way."

"What? This is the way out!" He said.

"They're coming after us, and we're running for the cars, right?"

"Well of fucking course we are! We need to get out of here and tell the authorities what's happened!"

"They'll be close behind," Rosa said, starting to breathe easier. "And there's some nice big open meadows between here and the cars. Great places to shoot us in the backs with that rifle." Farnsworth looked at her in horror, realizing she was right.

"We cross the stream here. The rocks are close enough together, we can hop across without leaving tracks, or just as bad, getting wet and leaving water residue. We go up the valley rather than down, and over into the next drainage," I said. "Hopefully, they'll continue down this valley and we can lose them."

"But we'll be going farther out into the wilderness, and they'll be able to make sure we can't use the cars then," Farnsworth said.

Rosa looked at him, and grimly smiled. "Cars won't do us any good with a bullet in our backs. If you want to go that way, we won't stop you, but you'd better flippin' sprint at the speed of sound."

Farnsworth considered for a moment. "You're right. If Cleeve can get us in line of sight, he can probably hit what he's aiming at with that scope. We need to move."

We shoved aside the clinging alders, and hopped out on the rocks crossing the rushing creek. It made my skin crawl to be in the open, but in less than a minute, we were across and carefully pushing our way through the brush on the other side.

I heard crashing through the brush and signaled for everyone to drop behind a big fir log that was lying parallel to the stream.

"Hurry, we need to catch up with those three, catch 'em where the valley widens out. One down the center, one of us on each flank!" It was Cleeve. They had been close on our heels, but their clumsy progress through the alders had given us just enough time to play our trick.

As they got farther away, we moved up the valley and kept close to, but not on, the trail that Three Feathers set his trap on earlier. We were three-quarters of the way to the top of the ridge when I called a halt.

"Let's stop and see if we can see them. I'd like to know if they're still following wild geese down the valley or not. Mason's not a great tracker, but he'll be able to see we're not going down the main trail."

"Yeah, but we're not going to the cars," Rosa said. "And if we were, we'd have to be idiots to stay on the trail, wouldn't we?"

"That's what I'm hoping he'll think. If he starts second guessing himself, maybe, they'll waste time trying to reacquire our trail."

"If I were them, and I thought we were heading to the cars," Rosa said, "I'd most likely just not worry about tracking and just try to outpace us. First one to the vehicles wins."

"Let's hope that's the way they go, then," Farnsworth said.

We sat in silence for a good twenty minutes, seeing no sign of our pursuit, and it was getting toward late afternoon. With a head gesture, I signaled to my companions that we should move up and over the ridge. We made haste for the top, and I was damn glad we were all in good shape.

We all breathed a sigh of relief when we were over the top and descending into the fading light of the new valley.

****

Darkness comes early in the northern latitudes in late September. We had barely hiked down amongst the trees when it began to be hard to see, the light turning everything to shades of dark blue and gray.

"It's likely to dip below freezing tonight, and we've got jack squat for gear," Farnsworth said. "We need to look for some kind of natural shelter, as I'm guessing a fire would be a very bad idea in our current situation."

"Mac still has his fanny pack on. I know he's got items in there we can use." Rosa told him.

"I've got a good headlamp," I said. "but I worry that those guys might be on a ridgeline above us. It's pretty bright, and I'm sure you could see it from a long distance."

"Hang on," Farnsworth said. I heard the jingle of keys, then a tiny red led flashlight came on. "I've had this little Photon light on my keyring for ages. Looks like it's going to come in handy. The red is pretty dim with any sort of distance."

We sat among some downed trees and emptied the contents of my old military butt pack onto my jacket. I'd taken it off and laid it out on the ground so nothing would be lost, and I felt the chill as soon as I removed it. I was lucky I still had my tactical vest on for a little extra warmth.

"Heavy duty space blanket. Nice!" Farnsworth said. "Got one of those in my pack, too. Which is still up on that plateau, unfortunately."

"We can wrap up in this and snuggle together. With three bodies, maybe we can generate enough reflected heat to not need a fire tonight," Rosa said. Her voice sounded tired.

"Are you okay?" I asked, "You took that shotgun blast full on. I was so scared you were dead, my heart almost exploded."

"I'm sure I'm one big bruise from stomach to ribs. Seemed like it took forever to get my breath again, but I don't think anything's broken. If you've got tweezers in your first aid kit, I might have to do a little buckshot mining on my right arm."

"I'm starting to think you might be from Krypton."

"Well," she smiled weakly, "I sure don't feel like no supergirl."

"You could've fooled me," Farnsworth said.

"Thanks for helpin' Mac get me outta there in one piece, Bill," she said. "Some folks would've just run away at full speed. Covered their own asses."

"I'm usually pretty good at ass covering, but I couldn't just leave you there to be murdered."

We were all silent for a moment, reliving the insane events of the day.

"I may have the solution to our fire problem," I said, breaking the gloomy introspection. The next thing I pulled out of the butt pack pile was a titanium Emberlit fold up twig stove. "If we're careful, I think we can burn small wood in this if we can find a sheltered spot. If we keep the flames small, the walls of the stove will keep it from throwing much light."

"Geez," Bill said. "I'm really glad you had that fanny pack. I've just got a few snack bars in my coat."

"As for food, I have a gallon Ziplock of trail mix. I also have this little primaloft vest which goes to Rosa to shore up the gaping hole in her jacket. Let's see, two USGI canteens with a steel canteen cup and some Aqua Mira drops. And a heavy duty trash bag. Two spare clips for my firearm. And my big knife on the back of my belt.

That's it, that's all she wrote."

"No matches?" Bill asked.

"No, I have a great survival kit back at my pack, for all the good it does us. But I have a flint sparker in my right sock. I'll get a fire going, don't worry."

"You keep a metal match… in your sock. Always? Or just in the woods."

"Ah. Pretty much always, and a tiny folder in my left sock." It was dark, but I could imagine his expression. "They saved my life once."

"Well," he said. "I have a lighter and matches, even a satellite phone, all sitting up in my pack next to the sheriff's final resting place. None of it here. So, if that's all we have, thank God we have it."

"Either of you have anything in your pockets?" I asked.

"Car keys, wallet, pocket knife," Farnsworth said. "Gloves in my coat pockets, pen… My .9mil… Oh! Hey! I had my monocular out, hoping to see Three Feathers first and stuffed it into my coat. Two Clif energy bars. That's it."

"I've got my folding knife, also my gloves and some almonds in a baggy for snacks. No wait. I lost the almonds when my coat was shredded by a shotgun," Rosa said, anger in her voice. "I also have your Glock, Mac."

"Keep it for the moment. Here's the extra magazines, too. If we get into another shoot out, I'd rather you have 'em," I said, pulling out the ammunition and handing it to her.

"What the fuck was Cleeve thinking?" Bill said, anger in his voice. "I knew something was wrong, but I had no inkling anything like that was gonna happen."

"It was crazy," I said. My mind snapped back to Rosa flying backward over the lip of the plateau. "But we can be damn sure, it was no misunderstanding."

"I think I might've hit Cleeve, but I'm not sure," Rosa said. "He told Belshaw to leave the three of us behind while they went after Three Feathers, maybe that was plan A, we'd just be witnesses."

"Looks to me like Plan B was 'Dead Men Tell No Tales,' no witnesses." I said. "But right now, the light is failing and we need shelter."

"They sure didn't hesitate on Plan B, did they?" Farnsworth said as he stood and gathered his things.

I gave Rosa the extra vest, and loaded my things back into the butt pack. We set about in earnest then, looking for a place we could set up out of sight, and out of the breeze that was starting to run down the valley. There was still enough light to make out some details, and within ten minutes, we'd found three boulders at the base of a rockslide. They had fallen in such a way that they left a triangular space between them, perfect for a windbreak. Now we just had to make the space more comfortable.

"Rosa, take my big knife to that grassy area and cut as much dry grass as you can stuff into this garbage sack," I told her. "Bill, if you could get some firewood, nothing bigger around than your finger, I'll see about making us all a bed to sleep in."

"I wonder if we should just risk your headlamp and try and hike outta here in the dark." Farnsworth said.

"Do you know this area that well?"

There was a moment of silence. "Actually, I don't. I've never been out in this area before, and my map's up there in my pack."

"Wait," Rosa said. "You're the enforcement guy out here and you don't know the area?"

"I know the campgrounds. I know the high use permit areas. I know the places where I usually give tickets," He said, somewhat defensively, "I have a general knowledge of the area, and I kinda know where we are, but I rarely have time to come this far into the back country. No one breaks the law out here."

"You realize the irony of that statement, right?"

"Painfully so. I'll get some firewood."

****

We woke well before dawn the next morning. I felt cold and stiff. I'm not sure any of us did more than doze, even though the adrenaline of the previous afternoon had worn off, and we all felt tired. I sparked our small stove to life, using tinder made from shredded inner fir bark, and we huddled around it, hands extended.

"How are you doin' this morning?" I asked Rosa, who had the space blanket still wrapped around her.

"Like I challenged Rhonda Rousey to a fight," she said. "I ache just about everywhere. Would you mind bringing me a peppermint mocha? I think that'll help."

"We have trail mix and boiled pine needle tea. Will that do?"

"Better than freezin' and starving."

I've actually been out on practice survival treks with less gear, but usually had more time to prepare a camp. We'd all slept shivering the previous night.

"We need to figure out a plan," Farnsworth said. He looked as haggard as I felt.

"I wish I'd spent a bit more time studying the map I had," I said, "This is not my home turf, and I just kind of fixated on the area where I was pretty sure Three Feathers was in."

"That poor man," Rosa said. "Right about now, I think we can say he definitely *was* framed."

"I'll bet you dollars to donuts it was Cleeve who shot that woman," Farnsworth said, "When he was sheriff, if his office was going to raid a meth house, they'd get there only to find out the occupants had cleared out just ahead of them. Never an arrest. Now, I know why."

"You think…" I started to say, "never mind, of course he's bad."

They both looked at me with a "Gee, ya think?" look on their faces.

"I'd just guess that having Belshaw win the sheriff's election kinda put a crimp in his operation. I think this whole trip was engineered just to get Dave out here, where he could be 'accidentally' killed in the line of duty," Farnsworth said, adding a few more sticks to the twig stove.

"Along with Three Feathers and all innocent bystanders and witnesses," Rosa said, a bitter edge to her voice. "Three Feathers would get the blame and it would all be a big tragedy, with heroic Cleeve and cronies taking down the bad man."

"Yeah."

I could feel it start to burn in my chest, that familiar anger, so heightened by the events of the previous year. The anger at those who think power gives them carte blanche to do whatever they want to whomever they want filled me.

"Fuck them," Rosa and Bill both looked up at the growling furious sound of my voice. "Like you said yesterday, Rosa, 'and the goat they rode in on,' the bastards. We are NOT dying out here."

"I like that idea," Farnsworth said.

"We're gonna get back, no matter how long it takes and no matter how hard the trail. We're gonna get back and when we do we are going to tell the world what they've done. We're going to exonerate Three Feathers' name. We're going to see that Belshaw has justice for his murder, and most of all, we're going to see these assholes behind bars for a very long time!"

Rosa smiled. "Damn straight," she said quietly.

"Well said, Mac," Farnsworth replied. "But that leaves the logistics of actually getting out of here."

"You live up here, Bill, what do you think?"

"We could go north into Canada, but that would be a trek, so would straight west. The North Cascades Highway is out that way, but it's a long ways through some rough country. I'd be up for that, but without gear and it's almost October, we'd be in a world of hurt if a snowstorm came in."

"We'll be in a world of hurt with a snowstorm any way we happen to go. And I saw how far out of the way this area is when we came up from the south."

"I'm thinking east. We could be in Okanogan County sooner than any of the other options except McClellan. Of course, McClellan is the closest point of civilization, but at this moment, Cleeve is the law there."

Rosa and I both looked at each other.

"Davies," she said.

"Bet he's not in Cleeve's pocket. Three Feathers was his cousin."

"Who?" Farnsworth said.

"Lincoln Davies. He's one of the Loman County deputies, but he was a new hire. He's also a Native American, and related to Jim Three Feathers. We had a talk with him, and I got the impression he wasn't that thrilled with his fellow deputies," I said.

"For that matter, there were several people in the town who didn't seem that thrilled with Cleeve. Maybe McClellan is the place to very carefully and discreetly make our way to," Rosa said.

"Okay guys, let's make that our overall plan," Farnsworth said, "but if we can find a dirt road with someone that'll get us a lift to the nearest government office, Forest Service, BLM, hell even an airstrip with a phone. If I can get a call out, I can get the FBI on this. We do that, and these slimeballs are done."

"Any chance of finding cell service out here?" Rosa asked.

"Slim to none. Even if you were on the highest peak out here, the nearest cell tower is very far away," Bill told her.

"Yeah," I said. "About what you said about telling the world... all the more reason for them to make sure the three of us stay out here forever. I think we've stayed in one spot long enough."

"Only if we want to live," Rosa replied.

CHAPTER SEVENTEEN

The Pasayten Wilderness is one of the most beautiful and least tramped areas of the United States. Under any other circumstances, I would have been entranced by the beauty I was seeing. The beautiful fall colored meadows now made me feel exposed and we certainly couldn't hang around the jewel-like lakes for any length of time.

The morning sun was only hitting the tops of the ridges, but we'd left our camp as soon as there had been enough light to walk without breaking our legs on obstacles.

Rosa, checked her phone as we came to a large open area. "Nothing, I'm gonna try to send a text to Gil. Sometimes you can get a text through even with a tiny amount of signal. My phone will hold the text 'til it finds something."

"Mine would just say 'undelivered' and 'too bad, so sad," Farnsworth said.

"If you leave it on all the time looking for service, Rosa, you'll kill the battery quick," I said.

"Once I do the text and hit send, and I'm sure it isn't going through, I'll shut it off and turn it on only when we hit likely spots. Think that'll work?"

"Can't hurt to try."

We had just filled my canteens at a small lake and were moving out when a thought occurred to me.

"Hey, guys? I see an opportunity here."

"Like what?" Farnsworth looked out over the narrow valley we were following downward.

"See up there, above the rockslide on the right? There's a game trail up there. The main trail here turns to rock, and it reminds me that Three Feathers did a lot to throw us off the trail. Maybe we should take a move from his playbook."

"Switch trails? But won't we have to come back to the main trail eventually?" Rosa asked.

"Maybe, or maybe we can stay on the ridgeline. It doesn't look too jagged. Either way, it might give their tracker a pain in the ass if they happened to find our trail. And from the valley we left, there was only one real path out besides the one back to the cars. They're probably following us by now."

"You think they're on our trail?" Rosa asked, alarmed.

"Stands to reason, and probably not that far behind. I'd guess that Teeg, and at least one other, are following us right now. The area around where we were was all broken backcountry, rockslides and cliffs. Even if we were getting tricky, they'd know that trying to go overland through that would be not only dangerous, but take us forever."

"And anyone with any sense is going to try to make it back to civilization and the authorities," Farnsworth added.

"Yeah," I said. "So the easier way would have been either back the way we came in, or the way that Three Feathers was originally going."

"Once we get a bit farther down on this trail, it'll possibly branch out to a couple different trailheads. We'll have that many more options and be that much harder to predict."

"Maybe we should just lay an ambush," Rosa said.

"I think I'd prefer to just get somewhere I can call in fellow federal agents. If we do that, Cleeve and his cronies will go from being official law enforcement to being wanted fugitives. I like that sound of that," Farnsworth told her.

"Maybe, though it might not be a bad idea to take another page from the Three Feathers' playbook, though," I said to them. "If I see a spot where we can lay a trap, even just to slow them down, and it won't take too much time or effort to set, then we'd better take the opportunity." They nodded.

"So, high road?"

"High road," Rosa replied.

"High road," Farnsworth agreed.

****

We climbed for two and a half hours before making it to the top of the ridge. The trails we'd gone up were definitely game trails, and the animals had not taken good engineering and ease of use for humans into consideration when they made them.

We tried to stay to the rocky bits, but there were spots where you either crossed open scree with lots of loose rock and soil, or you turned around and went back. Every time we crossed one of these slopes, I looked back at the tracks we were making and prayed they were hard to see from below.

"Okay, I need to sit for a few minutes," Farnsworth said, obviously winded. Sitting on flat rock, he pulled his jacket off and I saw it was reversible, the outer shell dark olive green, the liner blaze orange.

"Bill," Rosa said, "You wanna turn that bright orange away from the valley? Let's not be too easy to find, if it's not too much trouble."

"Ah, sorry," he said. "So what's the story with you two? Couple? Or just coworkers?"

"Coworkers, maybe working on couple," she replied. I felt a certain amount of elation to hear her say it.

"How about you, Bill?" I asked, "Married? Kids?"

"Do you see a ring on his finger, Mr. Awareness?" Rosa said, smiling.

"Honestly, when I meet another dude, I'm generally not checking out his rings or availability," I replied.

Farnsworth laughed at that. "I was married once. Two kids, Michael, who's about ten now, and Amber, my eight-year-old."

"They with their mom?" Rosa asked him.

"Yep. I see them during the summer and some holidays, but for the most part, they live with her." His face looked weary. "Goddamn. I sure hope I see them again. I don't give a rat's ass if I ever see their mother again, but I don't want to die without seeing my kids one more time."

That brought silence. I dug out the trail mix baggie, and we all made a good dent in the contents. We'd be foodless soon.

"Bill," Rosa said, "Can I borrow your monocular for a bit? I want to back track to that rocky point we just passed and see if I can see anyone behind us."

"Sure," he said. "Just give me a few minutes, and I'll be ready to roll."

"Beautiful country out here," I said to Farnsworth as Rosa trotted back down the game trail. "I wish we didn't have to run past it, constantly worrying about a bullet to the back." I looked after her and saw her glassing the valley we'd just came from.

"If we live through this, come up and I'll show you some great spots sometime, Mac."

"We *will* live..." looking back down the trail, I saw Rosa was gone. "Dammit! Where'd she go?"

"Bathroom break? After all, we have been staying pretty close together."

"If we were out here for a hike, I wouldn't worry, but under the circumstances, I better check."

I went back to where I'd last seen Rosa, and I was relieved to find her, a little farther down on a rock that jutted out over the mountainside. She was looking up the valley with the monocular, and when she heard me, she motioned for me to get down and join her.

"What is it?" I asked.

"Look up there, just past the lake," she said, handing me the monocular.

It took me a moment, looking through the single lens to find what she meant. There was a figure coming down the trail we'd left and he appeared to be carrying a rifle.

"Mason," I said. "I can tell from the way he sways side to side a bit as he walks."

"Shit!"

"Guess he's a better tracker than I thought."

CHAPTER EIGHTEEN

"I still think you should've just let me ambush him."

"Rosa, first of all, there's a chance you might not get him with your first shot."

She gave me a flat look.

"Second of all, he has a rifle, probably that M-4 carbine. He 'out-ranges' you. He can hit you with the rifle a lot farther away than you can hit him with a .45."

"So, you're the Natural Camouflage Expert. Camo me up, and I'll ambush him twenty feet from the side of our trail!"

"Hey. Guys," Farnworth interrupted, "like I said before, the best plan is to just avoid our pursuers all together. Let's get out of here and tell the authorities what's happened. Any time we come in contact with Cleeve's bunch, even from ambush, there's that much more chance things won't go our way."

"I'd say they already haven't gone our way," Rosa said.

"We stick to the plan," he replied. "We get out, we tell what we saw, we all go home alive."

"I especially like that last part," I said. "When we come to a better spot, I'll figure out a better way to throw Mason off the trail. Workin' on a couple ideas for that, just need the right setup."

We were moving on the ridge line and we were fortunate in that while the side sloped away steeply, the top of the ridge was a rolling walkway of alpine plants and stunted spruce trees. The mountain on either side had started to drop away precipitously into steep hillsides with minimal trees due to regular snow slides.

In some places, we were walking above sheer naked cliff faces. I was watching for any way to get into the valley to the north, filled with trees as it was. The valley we'd come from opened up into a series of meadows, beautiful to hike in, but not so easy to move through and not be seen.

We'd probably hiked another six or so miles when Farnsworth had to call a halt again.

"I'm sorry guys. Guess sitting at a desk for half of my workday isn't doing much to keep me in shape."

"S'okay, Bill," Rosa said, "Mac an' I have been training for some of the local running events in our area."

"Doesn't hurt that you two are at least ten years younger, either."

"I dunno man," I said, "The last race we ran in, Rosa came in number twenty-five out of one-fifty. The guy who came in twenty-sixth was forty-five years old."

"Thanks, Mac," he laughed as he said it, "thanks a shitload. I tell you though, an experience like this really makes you do some re-evaluating on how you're living your life. You keep telling yourself you have time, all the time in the world, and the next thing you know, you don't."

Rosa looked at me with an enigmatic expression, possibly wanting me to say something encouraging.

"Bill," I said. "We're gonna get out of this. Stay strong and we'll beat these assholes."

"I noticed," Rosa said, "that you didn't mention where you came in on that race, Mac."

Bill looked at me expectantly.

"Aw... sheesh," I said, "No allowances for male pride here. I came in... thirty-sixth."

He laughed. "Well, I would have come in a hundred and forty-ninth, I think."

****

I wasn't going to lie, Bill's need to stop frequently had me a little worried. When I'd seen Teeg Mason through the monocular, he hadn't been carrying the large pack he'd had earlier, and was moving much faster than when we'd come into this wilderness. He'd probably be on our heels if we dawdled much, unless he was in worse shape than Bill.

The rest of the day was one long slog of climbing over blown down trees or navigating rockslides with boulders the size of dump trucks, and we all looked down on the relatively open valley floor with envy. For all of Bill's talk of being out of shape, I guessed that most of the people I knew would have folded under this kind of punishment. Bill trooped on.

The human body, however, was not built in the image of the mountain goat. Most animals in the wild tended to try to find the easiest route, not wanting to burn more calories that absolutely needed. The goats seemed to be another story, with trails that went to some of the craziest routes. Following these trails was often an exercise in frustration.

Late afternoon found us arriving at a cliff face. We could see a nicely treed area on the other side, where, if we could find a flat spot, we might be able to make a halfway decent camp and get off the exposed hillside we'd been crossing.

"Looka that ledge," Rosa said pointing to where rock had fallen off the face at one time. "Think we can get across there?"

"It's doable, if we're careful," Bill told her. "We'll just need to take it slow, and not get cocky. If we edge out, face to the cliff we should be okay."

"It's at least a foot wide at most points," I said, "but it does slope a bit towards the edge."

"Well," he said. "we can't stay here. It's getting close to sunset, and we're out in the open"

"We have to try. We ain't exactly flying along here," Rosa said.

"As long as we don't fly off the cliff."

We crept along the precipice, moving at a snail's pace, and of course, like an idiot, I had to look over the edge. It was a long way down, a LONG way down, with not much between us and the rocks below. I took a deep breath and kept on inching sideways toward the trees.

After approximately forever, we were across and heaving sighs of relief. The traverse would fall under what I called an emergency maneuver, AKA very risky without being roped off. Technical climbers might poo-pooh my nervousness, but I was far from a proficient rock climber.

We all sat on a spruce log and nibbled on the last of my trail mix. I was chagrined to see both Bill and Rosa seemed to not have been that worried by the height of the ledge. I never thought of myself as having a fear of heights, but that crossing had made me more than nervous.

"Hey!" Rosa said, "Do you hear that?"

"Sounds like a helicopter?" I replied.

"Yeah. Oh damn. Could that be Cleeve?"

"No," Bill said. "Loman County is too small and poor to have a sheriff's chopper. It's more likely a fire spotter or maybe Park Service a little off their range."

"Seems late in the year to be a fire spotter," Rosa said.

"You'd be surprised," Bill told her, taking off his jacket. He turned it inside out so the orange lining was showing.

"A signal?" I asked.

"This could be our chance," he replied. "If we can get their attention, I bet we can get them to land in the valley. Then, we just have to find a way down and hopefully have a ride out of here. I'm willing to ride on a frickin' landing strut if I have to."

"You think it might be a government copter?" Rosa asked.

"You'd have to have a special permit to fly this low over the wilderness if you were a civilian. Needless to say, Forest Service and Park Service helicopters aren't under the same constraint. What little air traffic there is up here flying this low, is going to be government," he said, starting to edge back onto a wider spot on the ledge.

A few moments later, we saw a white and green Jet Ranger helicopter coming down the valley. Bill grabbed a crack in the rock face with his left hand and began furiously waving his jacket with his right.

"Can't make out the lettering on it yet," Rosa said and I saw she had Bill's monocular to her eye.

"Come on out here, you two!" Bill yelled, "The more motion we make, the more chance they'll see us! We've got one shot at this!"

I started forward, but Rosa hip-blocked me.

"What?"

"They've seen him," she said. "Let's hang back a moment."

Rosa was my security advisor, and she had great instincts. I stopped where I was.

We stood at the edge of the trees while Bill frantically waved the jacket, and the helicopter slowed, then turned end for end, now facing up the valley. It began to move sideways towards our hillside and Rosa continued to watch it through the monocular.

"Mac," she said, her voice rising, "That's not a government chopper. The logo on the side says Rightway Logging."

"What's a logging helicopter doing in a wilderness area?"

"Oh, SHIT!" she yelled, taking her eye away from the eyepiece. She turned toward where Farnsworth stood on the ledge and screamed, "BILL! Get in here! Now! That's Cleeve!"

Adrenalin spiked through me as I tried to make out our enemy in the now open door of the helicopter. Rosa motioned furiously for Bill to come back to the trees, and he looked perplexed. He hadn't made out what she was saying over the noise of the helicopter.

I motioned toward the chopper and screamed at the top of my lungs, "CLEEVE!"

He got it that time and looked with horror at the approaching craft. Farnsworth started sidestepping toward the trees again with determination, using the vertical split in the rock for support.

And then, the rock face behind him was painted red.

I heard the crack of the rifle a half second after I saw the blood spatter behind him, and Bill just stood there a moment, looking at me with a surprised expression. The jacket slipped from his fingers, and the winds from the approaching helicopter blew it out over the valley. His feet slid out from under him, dangling for a moment off the sloping ledge and he started to slip forward. One moment he was staring at me, as if somehow I could still save him, then he slid out and gravity took over.

He was gone.

We stood staring for a moment, and I guess that it was the jostling of the air currents from the copter that saved our lives. For the second time in two days, I felt a bullet go by my head so close that the shock wave rustled my hair.

"Move!" Rosa yelled! "We're on a bullseye here!"

We dodged deeper into the firs, and began making our way upwards towards the top of the ridge until we found a tangle of blow-downs to hide in. Watching the helicopter circle, we knew we only had to wait them out: craft like these drink fuel like Great Aunt Tilley sucked down Manhattans. As the sun began to go below the distant mountains, Cleeve and his pilot gave up, and the helicopter flew off toward the east.

CHAPTER NINETEEN

That evening, with spirits drained, we moved into another valley, that thankfully, was dropping in the direction we wanted to go.

"Here," I told Rosa, "We'll sleep here."

We had found a huge old Ponderosa pine, with limbs reaching the ground on all sides, and a huge amount of long pine needles underneath. It was sitting in a flat spot a few hundred feet above the valley floor. I found six downed saplings, not hard with all the lodgepole pines nearby. I made bed rails at the base of the tree, backing them with stakes carved with my big knife, and using the garbage sack, I poured the long pine needles in, bag after bag. Soon we had a serviceable, if somewhat prickly mattress.

"I am so tired," Rosa said, and I empathized. We were physically and emotionally drained, and to be honest, our morale couldn't get much lower. Underlying it all was the feeling that Bill's fate was a preview of our own.

"We've got two energy bars left," I said. "Eat 'em now, or in the morning, you think?"

"Gonna be hard enough to stay warm tonight. We'll probably need some fuel."

"Gonna need fuel tomorrow too," I replied. "How about we split one tonight and have the other for breakfast."

"Sî, esta bueno."

We wrapped up in the tarp/space blanket like a double burrito and Rosa moved against me and laid her head on my chest.

"Smells like snow coming in," I said, wearily.

"You can smell weather?"

"Kinda. Smells like cold. Smells like the realm of the winter queen. The breeze is carrying it down from the north."

"I like that. I'll think of that whenever I see snow now."

"Poetic notions, all part of the service, ma'am. No charge."

Rosa said nothing for a while, and I wondered if she'd gone to sleep. Myself, I wondered if I'd ever be able to sleep again. Bill's face floated up into my consciousness every time I tried to drop off.

"He'll never see his kids again," Rosa said. Not asleep either.

"Yeah. I can't stop seeing his face, hoping I'm gonna come out to him and somehow keep him from dying. It was my fault, you know."

"What!?" Rosa raised to look me in the eye. "How the hell is Cleeve murdering that man your fault, Mac? Estupido!"

"I was the one who was so damn clever I got us on that open hill side. I was the one who was going to throw them off our track, and then got us on those talus slopes where we couldn't hide our trail. My fault."

"Jesus, Mac!" If we'd stayed out on that open valley floor, Cleeve would have caught all three of us out in the open. There'd be three bodies then, and the shit heads would be back at the ranch celebrating with a beer while los coyotes gnawed on our faces!"

"I should just…" I choked, "..I should be better than this."

"Mac, just… don't. Don't do this to yourself. Bill's death is not on you. If he hadn't decided that Cleeve couldn't possibly have a helicopter and waved him in, we'd all be here and still heading out. Do *not* give despair a foothold in your heart. We need… I… need for you to get us out of here. You gotta stay strong."

"Cleeve's a former ranger…"

"And you're the best person out here, in places like this, I've ever seen, and I was in the marines. Now it's down to will and strategy," she said. "I say we figure out a way to kick his ass. I say you're better than him. Him and all his asshole deputies."

"Yeah," I said. "Yeah, goddam it. No more Mr. and Ms. Nice Guy!"

"Damn right. We know that little weasel Teeg Mason is tracking us. We need to mess that guy up."

"Yep. First chance we get."

****

It wasn't long thereafter, that I heard Rosa begin a soft little snore against my chest. Sleep wasn't coming as easy for me. For all my talk of dealing with our pursuers, I still kept thinking about Bill Farnsworth and if there was anything I could have done differently.

Rosa was right. I needed to get my head in the game, but the only people I had ever seen die were the ones who had actively been trying to put a bullet in me. Bill had been different. He was a good man, and if mutual distress can cause friendships, then I definitely called him friend.

Rosa had been in the Middle East, as an MP, supposedly not a frontline combatant. But she'd also been stationed in areas where when a horde of frothing insurgents tried to overrun a position, everyone picked up a rifle and fought. And saw friends die.

"One," I breathed, watching the starry skies through the pine limbs.

"Two," I whispered quiet as a breeze on the second breath. Bills face tried to come to me again.

"Three." Another breath.

"Four."

After ten minutes, just counting my breath, Bill decided my mind could be better occupied trying to sleep and left me alone.

At around two in the morning, I was awakened by Rosa rising suddenly.

"What?" I whispered, "Did you hear something?"

"I had a dream, a bad one. La Pesadilla," she said quietly, "It was you, not Farnsworth on the ledge. I watched you go over and I couldn't move to stop it. I was frozen in place."

"It was just a dream, sweetheart. Just a dream. I'm okay, still alive."

"My heart is beating so fast."

"It's all right, now. It's all…" I found myself interrupted by warm soft lips. The pressure started lightly then increased, and as a dainty tongue touched my teeth, I realized I was the one whose heart was now beating fast. Rosa's hips were grinding against my hipbone and our kiss grew strong and fierce. Her hand on my chest began to move downward across my stomach, farther down until finally touching the sizable bulge in the front of my pants. She began rubbing it and I gasped.

"I... I thought we were," I panted, "going to take it slow?"

"Oh baby, we might not be alive tomorrow. Just think, what things was Bill holding off on?" she said, her breath coming fast. "I don't want to lose you. I don't want to go out without having done this with you, one more time!"

"We're gonna make it—" Rosa interrupted me again with an even deeper kiss, and I forgot what I was going to say.

Kissing her and holding her tightly, I turned on my side toward her and reached around to start squeezing her muscular butt. Her thigh rubbed against my leg and I felt her fingers fumbling with the buttons on my fly. I felt a rush of sensation as she reached past underwear to find and stroke my almost painfully hard penis.

I was kissing her neck when I realized there were a few logistic problems that lovers have whenever trying to go from clothed to unclothed, but ours were complicated by coats and ballistic vests. And what seemed like a thousand damn buttons.

Finally, I was kissing her collar bones and there was no clothing to get in the way of my going farther down. I worked my way down over nipples hard, erect and crinkled, past a flat stomach, over smooth hips and farther down to a place salty, wet, and warm. My tongue wiggled wildly over soft parts and Rosa, back arching, had to stick her hand in her mouth to keep from crying out.

Finally, she couldn't stand any more and pulled at me to move me up to lie on top of her, between her spread legs. A moment's adjustment and I felt myself slide into a warm, wet and wonderful place. This brought its own problems. I had pretty much been celibate (not by choice) for some time now, and this explosion of slippery pleasure threatened to end this incredible moment early. It was only through superhuman mental reciting of the Seahawks win-loss stats that premature catastrophe was averted.

Fortunately for me, Rosa was almost as close. As I moved my hips forward, she began to shudder and thrust her hand back to her mouth. Even muffled, the sounds of her moans and whimpers drove me wild and I increased my pace, until in a huge spasm, her hips lifted me off the ground. Her back arched and the hand couldn't stifle her cry of pleasure. I felt her clench me and that was it, Seahawks be damned. I exploded like a supernova and the aftershocks that followed were almost as intense.

We lay there in each other's arms, feeling that warm relaxation that follows a great moment like this. For a short time, we were able to forget how much trouble we were in; we were able to just be. Just her and me together.

If I had died in then and there, I would have died happy.

****

It's very romantic to sleep nude together, but it wasn't long 'til we were scrambling in the cold to get our clothes on. Between the clothes, the space blanket and a foot of pine needles laying over us we were able to get a decent night's sleep.

I woke the next morning, before dawn, and looked out from our hiding place over the valley, screened through a latticework of limbs. I felt something cold hit my half exposed face, and saw one of my fears confirmed.

"Rosa," I said. "It's snowing."

CHAPTER TWENTY

We sat around the titanium twig stove, heating a canteen cup of pine needle tea for a warm up drink.

"So what does this snow mean for us?" Rosa asked, handing me half of the last energy bar.

"It means it's going to be damn hard to not leave a visible trail as we do our best to get the hell out of here. When there's just plants and brush to move through a tracker has to take his time to not lose the trail. In the snow, ol' Teeg'll probably be able to track us at a jog."

"So what do we do?"

I looked at her and sighed. "We try to stay out ahead of him, and stay close enough to the trees that our trail doesn't stand out from the air."

"And if Teeg is radioing ahead to Cleeve and his pilot," she said, "they can probably figure out places to jump us with the helicopter. Not good."

"Not good, indeed. It's even more imperative that we, and I *never* thought I'd be the one saying this, take out the tracker. But for now, we need to drink this tea and get moving. We need to try to get a decent lead so we'll have time to see opportunities for defensive action."

Rosa took out my Glock and checked the rounds in the loaded magazine.

"Maybe we should go on the offensive. Move back and see if we can find a spot to shoot him from."

"My gut says no. We need to lay a trap. Teeg Mason almost

blundered into a fairly obvious trap that Three Feathers laid, and if we can nail him with one, we don't even have to take the risk of him shooting back."

"Hit the other side without taking any hits ourselves?" Rosa said. "I can work with that."

We drank our tea quickly, and while Rosa reloaded my butt pack, I listened carefully to what the valley was telling me. Chickadees cavorted in amongst the spruce. A buck across the valley was peacefully looking for the last of the tender leaves before they all fell and were covered.

"I think we're okay at the moment," I said, "Let's get this show on the road."

Rosa handed me my butt pack and I untangled the Y-shaped suspenders and shrugged into it. We moved out, staying farther up on the hill, paralleling the path of the valley. Even with snow, Teeg was going to have to work for it.

"Mac, do you think there might be any kind of legitimate search going on for us?" Rosa asked.

"We've only been out a few days, and for all the outside world knows, we're still out tracking Three Feathers. Besides, when wilderness searches are initiated, it's usually at the call of local sheriff."

"Who is now Dominic Cleeve," she said, a flat tone in her voice.

"Yep."

We trekked on, taking the least obvious paths and the snowfall gradually increased until the air was filled with big white fluffy flakes. Even the trees around us started to seem indistinct. The deeper it got, the more our trail showed, and I was hoping the snowstorm would obliterate our tracks before Mason could catch up.

"I wonder what Teeg's deal is," I said. "He took a shot at me as I was going after you, and it looked like he was really upset about it. Holmes and Cleeve, on the other hand, were cold as ice. They didn't bat an eye at trying to kill multiple people."

"Probably because to those two, we're not people," Rosa replied, climbing over a downed tree trunk. "We're just objects that need to be removed for their plans to move forward. It could be as cold, cut, and dried as that."

"Yeah. Teeg didn't seem that way, though."

"That stuff about not wanting to get to know you, maybe it wasn't about him thinking you were gay." She said, "Maybe it was him knowing he was assigned to slaughter you and not wanting to make it any harder on himself."

"He seemed like a man who's got himself in deep and doesn't know how to get out."

Rosa whirled on me. "Mac, don't even think of going all empathetic on that son of a bitch. You told me yourself that if you hadn't moved when you did, he would have shot you right between the eyes. I don't care what his *mierda de cabeza* motivation is, if we get the chance, he's toast. Whether he feels bad about what he's done is not relevant. He's tracking us, and I'm guessing that's part of how Cleeve found us. He's at least part of the reason Bill is dead at the bottom of that cliff."

"Yeah," I said, "don't worry. I'm not going all Stockholm Syndrome. I am watching for any way I can see to fuck him up."

"Glad to hear it. Hey, a game trail! Think we dare to follow it for a while?"

We had emerged from a forested tangle to a fairly clear pathway. That it was a flat pathway on the side of the hill led me to believe that it was probably elk that had made it, the big ungulates were almost as good at trail making as their two legged neighbors. It followed the same direction as the main trail on the valley floor. We wandered another mile, making good time and feeling good to just be out of the debris ridden undergrowth when I found something very strange. A coyote track.

"No way," I said, stopping to examine it closely.

Rosa came back looking down at what I was seeing. With exasperation in her voice, she said, "Mac, we don't have time to be looking at animal tracks for God's sake!"

"This track, it can't be the same..." I said. The track was a large male coyote, a right rear track. The outside toe on the track bent out at almost a forty-five degree angle from the paw. It was exactly the right size.

"Mac, let's go."

"All right, but I'd swear this is the same coyote that hangs around Uncle Gil's farm."

She gave me a 'whatever, who cares look,' and we started down the trail.

Either I knew a lot less about animal tracks than I thought, or that particular characteristic of an overlarge male coyote's right rear foot was much more common than logic would have one believe. If it had been under other circumstances, there's little on Earth that would have pried me away from this mystery, but Rosa was right. This was no time for scientific or artistic inquiry.

We moved through the trees at almost a light jog, the trail being that flat. The snow was starting to deepen, but breaks were appearing in the clouds, and occasional patches of sunlight would brighten parts of the hillside. We were almost to a rockslide, where we would have to slow down and cross through broken rock when I found the same tracks again. I couldn't help myself, I had to stop.

"Mac! For pity's sake, we're tryin' to get out ahead..." Her voice trailed off and I looked up at her, then looked where Rosa was looking.

He was standing in the middle of the trail.

****

I swear to you, it was The King, the huge male coyote that was always showing up at Uncle Gil's, but it couldn't be. That was over a hundred miles away. But... he had the same scar on the left side, and when he turned to look directly into my eyes, the same mocking expression. It couldn't be him.

But somewhere, deep in my gut, I knew it was. A shiver went down my spine.

"Wow. That guy's bold," Rosa said.

"It's..." I almost couldn't get the words out. "It's him! King Coyote."

"Can't be." Rosa knew who I was talking about. She'd suffered through several track-based 'geeking out' conversations between Ed and me, and at one time, I had actually pointed out the furry devil to her, watching us through the sagebrush. She didn't sound too sure of herself.

The coyote turned away from us then. He looked up the hill, toward the top edge of the rockslide then pointedly looked back at me. He then looked up the hill again, and back at me. The message was clear and I turned that way to see what he seemed to be showing us.

As I scanned the hill above, an opening in the clouds lit up the rockslide and for a moment, I saw something uphill reflect a flash of light. I pointed it out to Rosa, and we both crouched immediately. I looked toward the coyote again…

Gone.

I saw the tracks where he had stood, and even from twenty feet away, I could see there were no tracks moving away in the snow beyond where he'd sat.

None.

****

Forty-five minutes later, Rosa and I had back-tracked, then cut up the hill to come out above where I had seen the momentary reflection.

It was rough going, up a steep hill over rocks and logs covered with snow and the fact that we'd only had half an energy bar each didn't help matters, but we were more than motivated.

If what I thought was causing the glint we'd seen in the fleeting patch of sunlight was right, we couldn't proceed forward down the valley. There was no cover, even on the valley floor for several hundred yards, even with the heavy wet snowfall dropping all around us. After all the climbing, we were above where I had seen the reflections, looking down on the rockslide.

"There," I whispered, so softly it was little more than a breath. Rosa's gaze followed where I pointed. Below us on a small shelf caused by overlapping boulders was a rough square of white. Closer inspection showed it to be a camouflaged tarp, maybe a poncho, now almost entirely white with snow. A gun barrel, jutted from under the square, underneath its own protective cloth. It looked like it belonged to a high caliber hunting rifle, and I was pretty sure it would have a long-range scope attached for sniping.

Had Rosa and I simply continued across the landslide as we had been doing, we would probably both have large holes in important parts of our anatomies by this time.

"Hijo de puta!" she whispered.

"Son of a bitch, indeed," I agreed.

"This one we must take out. But we have to get close enough to even the odds," Rosa said.

"I wish we still had Bill and his nine mil. If two of us were shooting, one could distract while the other got close enough to take the shot."

"Let's focus on what is, not what we wish," Rosa said quietly. "Do you think you can get above him without attracting his attention?"

"Yeah, I'm pretty good at moving quietly," I said, trying to see things positively, "and now, we've both got enough snow on our shoulders and hats that it's practically camouflage."

"Go then, and once you're in position, I'll see if I can put a round into that tarp. Maybe I'll get lucky, but even if I wound him, you're probably gonna have to drop down on him and do that Karate thing of yours."

Sensei Dade's words came back to me: *Stop being so predictable, Mac*.

"I'm not real crazy about that idea. Me, going hand to hand against a rifle is *real* iffy. Can *you* get above him quietly?"

"Yeah, maybe. That tarp he's under hides everything going on above him. But the rocks above him block my shot unless he stands. Why?"

"See the boulder to his right? If I can get to that, I can send a few rocks his way, and I bet he'll come out to play if that happens. I drop behind the boulder, you shoot him as he comes to get me."

"I don't like it. What if I can't get a shot?" There was a tiny furrow of worry between Rosa's dainty brows.

"You're more likely to get a shot than I would be able to cover thirty feet silently and attack a guy with a rifle, hand to hand, and come out on top."

"Well. When you say it like that…"

****

It put my heart in my throat a few times, watching her navigate the snow-slicked boulders to where she needed to be. A boulder field on a steep hill was not a good place to have a mishap. She slipped twice and almost took some bad falls. In fifteen minutes though, she was in position just a stone's throw above our sniper.

I could see then, that there was no way she could get a shot into him while he was lying down. There were a couple of truck-sized boulders that blocked the shot. To shoot him while he was prone would mean moving farther up the hill, taking a longer shot through a snow storm. We could have risked it, but the chance of a miss could be the end of us if our shooter was really good with that rifle.

'C'mon, baby," I whispered to myself. She replaced the half-empty magazine in the Glock with one of the full ones on her belt. I saw her fiddle with the gun for a moment, then she signaled she was ready.

I worked my way to the nearest boulder on the little plateau the shooter hid on and looked around for a rock of decent size to throw. It was harder than expected, as most of the smaller rocks and boulders had fallen down into gaps between the larger ones, but eventually I found a shard about the size of a small laptop. Rather than trying to throw it overhand, I spun my whole body and lobbed the stone like a discus over the boulder I between the ambusher and myself.

My aim was better than expected.

The rock flew true and actually hit the shape under the poncho a glancing blow. The reaction was explosive.

"What the fuck?" The poncho erupted upward, and Holmes came out from underneath, rifle at the ready. He was packing an older lever action rifle with duct tape on the stock, but the scope it carried looked brand new and expensive. Before he could see me, I dropped behind the boulder and and looked beyond him to where I could see Rosa lining up her shot through the falling snow. She shifted her weight to try and get a firm shooting stance, but just as she fired, Holmes slipped on the snowy rock and her shot went awry.

"You bitch!" Holmes screamed at her, rapidly firing back with the lever action rifle. "You ain't gonna have long to be sorry, 'cause you gonna be dead!"

Rosa dropped down behind the boulder she'd been using to hide behind, and bullets peppered the area around her. She waited, hoping Holmes would run out of ammo, but peeking around my own boulder, I could see he had a side arm too, and if she wasn't lucky, she could be hit by a ricochet from one of the weapons. Gunfights are not something to go into lightly.

I slipped out from behind the boulder and moved toward him, praying he wouldn't look my way. Holmes seemed to have forgotten in his outrage at being shot at, that Rosa was not alone in this fiasco.

"You may as well c'mon out, stupid. I got a quota of people that I gotta make dead, and now you're at the top o' the list!" He was in a fury and sent a few more shots up the hill, nicely covering the sound of my approach.

Holmes realized I was there when I was less than eight feet from him and ready to attack with knife drawn. He was able to deflect my blade with the rifle barrel, but only served to open up his belly to a strong front kick. As he grunted from the impact, I punched him hard in the right bicep. Letting go of the knife, I grabbed the rifle and gave it a strong yank.

His numbed arm couldn't hang on to it.

"Shit!" Holmes yelled as I pulled it away and tried to cross draw the pistol at his belt with his left hand. I didn't even bother reversing the rifle, instead I slammed the end of the stock into his forehead, sending him reeling back over the slippery rock ledge. The results were predictable.

Arms whirling, he went off the ledge and out of sight. I heard a thud a moment later, and moving forward, rifle at ready, I saw him on another boulder twelve or thirteen feet below. The pistol he'd been trying for was nowhere to be seen, and I guessed it had fallen down between the rocks. He lay there, barely moving, and groaning.

"Rosa! Are you okay?"

"I'm okay," her voice came down the hill. "Did you get Holmes?"

"Ooooh yeah. He's definitely gotten."

"I'll be right down. These rocks are incredibly slick."

She was right. I carefully climbed down to our assailant, trying to both keep an eye on him and not slip between the rocks myself. Holmes was lying face up on a relatively flat boulder, snowflakes falling on his upturned face. I could see he was still conscious, but looked to be in a great deal of pain.

"Well," I said, kneeling a few feet away, "that little ambush didn't go according to plan, did it?"

"Awww shit," his voice was strained, "I think I broke my hip when I landed. Aw God, it hurts." He squirmed and his left hand clawed at the rock. "Need something for the pain. Please!"

"Gee. My first aid kit's back with my pack. You know, at that spot where you three started murdering people?"

"Got Vicodin in… my pack. Please! For the pain!"

I heard a noise behind me, and Rosa was there with a small military type pack. She was folding up the poncho and the poncho liner blanket he'd been lying under. She had a foldable foam pad under one arm and was rifling through the pack's contents.

"His gear ought to make our life a bit easier out here," she said.

"Is there a first aid kit? He's got some painkiller in there and he says his hip's broken."

"Is it?" she asked. "Let's check." Rosa walked over and nudged the deputy with her boot, jerking his whole body. His scream would have made Torquemada proud.

"Hunh," she said, handing me my knife, "I guess he's not faking."

I dug through the pack, and handed Holmes a bottle of pills and his water bottle.

"You sure we want to help this *pendejo*?" Rosa asked, looking down at Holmes with disdain.

"Just the pain pills and the water. We're taking the rest. Thanks for the supplies, Holmes."

"Wait, you… you can't just leave me here, unable to move.. In a fuckin' snow storm. Please, help me!"

Rosa and I looked at each other, incredulous.

"Are you shitting me?" I asked.

"You were up here on this hill to bushwhack us," Rosa said, "to leave us facedown in the snow. And you have the *cojones* to ask us to help you?"

"True narcissistic personality," I said.

"Textbook," Rosa replied.

We were ready to take our leave, and seeing that, Holmes was able to calm down enough to argue.

"I can help you. You make it outta here, Cleeve'll just say you two were in it with Three Feathers. You'll go to jail for all them murders!"

Rosa rolled her eyes. "So, we just came up to this place, having never met anyone here, and decided to kill off the sheriff and a federal law officer, just for grins. Yeah. No one will ever question that."

I had everything stuffed into the small backpack, and was searching for Holmes' handgun. I finally saw it, in between the gaps in some of the boulders, but it was so far down, I couldn't quite reach it. I figured if I couldn't, then there was no way Holmes could. Nonetheless, I didn't mention it in front of him.

"Rosa, let's hit the trail."

"You can't leave me!" Holmes pleaded.

I whispered to Rosa, "Teeg is tracking us. He'll find Holmes."

"That's a relief. I was *so* worried about him," Rosa said. "Let's go."

We left amidst Holmes' sobbing like a bleating goat, being unaware that Mason was en route.

But we were sadly aware of it. I knew Rosa had been tempted to just finish Holmes off, understandably to reduce the number of murderers after us.

"So . . . We didn't kill him." I said.

"I didn't think it was in our best interest."

"Not in our best interest to kill that asshole who wouldn't have thought twice about killing us?"

"Holmes' injuries might actually slow Mason down." Rosa said. "Surely he won't leave Holmes lying there, they're on the same team."

"True."

"Last but not least, in the offhand chance that we survive, the sad truth is that we could actually be tried for murder if we had killed the man attempting to kill us." She shrugged. "You people have funny laws."

"Yeah. Once we got past the wild west days, things went downhill."

"The burden of proof would be on us to show that we had acted in self-defense."

"Got it." I forced myself to stop questioning things that would be better left to another day and to focus on priority one. How to stay alive.

CHAPTER TWENTY-ONE

"Maybe we should have at least left him the poncho and liner though, covered him with them. The snow's coming down pretty hard," I said. It had taken us a while to get off the rockslide, and now we were trying to make up time on the game trail.

"Are you kidding me? He's lucky I didn't strip him out of that down jacket and those insulated pants he was wearing. If he'd broken his neck instead of his hip, I would have."

"That coat's insulation," I told her, "is gonna get pretty wet pretty fast."

"MacKenzie Crow, that man was there to kill us. Save your fretting for someone who deserves it."

"Yeah. I guess this isn't really the time to walk in someone else's shoes."

"Ya think?"

We pushed on down the valley, and looking back, I could only hope that the snowstorm would quickly cover the obvious trail we were leaving. If it were any other situation, I'd worry we were going to get lost in the heavy snowfall, but all we could do at this point was follow the valley.

"Hey," Rosa interrupted my worrying, "I'm really running low on fuel. Let's stop under that big pine up ahead for a minute and see if there's any food in that pack."

We were in luck. Holmes was a man who liked to snack, and along with a roast beef sandwich from a local grocery, there were several energy bars, an orange, and even a can of Coke. For two active people running through snowy mountains on half an energy bar each, it was a feast. I was relieved we weren't going to have to eat the inner bark of the local pines to gain our carbohydrates.

We sat in a small area of pine needles where the snow couldn't reach and watched the storm swirling around us. It was beautiful, the fat flakes drifting to the ground, set against the dark conifers. Any other time, I would have been enchanted, but now, it was daunting and the snow was already ankle deep. I wondered how far we were from anything civilization offered that could do us any good.

"Hmmm," Rosa said, looking at her cell phone, "I can't tell if my text went or not. It doesn't say 'delivered,' but it doesn't say 'pending' any more either. Looks like my battery isn't gonna last much longer, though."

"I thought you had a good charge."

"I turned it on when we were on the ridgeline with Bill, hoping at that height I'd get something, anything, for cell service." She looked embarrassed. "I forgot, with everything that happened, to shut it off."

"Gee," I smiled ruefully as I said it. "I can't imagine why you'd forget. It's not like anything out of the ordinary has been going on."

"That might be a very telling commentary on the lives we lead. But dammit, I have a small charger in the pack we left behind. Fat lot of good it's doing us now. How's your phone?"

I pulled it out of my coat pocket. "Half charge. It was just under three-quarters when we started. I guess you're gonna lose some power even when it's turned off. Every time I turn it on, though, it starts searching for service and the battery goes down that much faster."

"The cold could have something to do with it, too. Turn it off again and keep it in an inner pocket. If we can get in line of sight with a cell tower, or just find service we can call for help."

"Speaking of cold, maybe we better get going again. I need to generate a little heat, and we really have no idea how far behind Teeg Mason is."

****

A never ending swirl of white flakes fell in front of our eyes, the white carpet halfway to our calves. I had to keep checking the trees to make sure we were moving east, even though we had little option but to follow the valley that we had been in. The ridge lines were even tougher going, with deeper snow than in the valleys and were a sure bet for a bad fall. We stayed low.

"Mac," Rosa said. "It's not letting up. Are... are we gonna make it out of here?"

It was the first crack in her usual steely imperturbability I'd seen since we'd started this whole mess. It was time to rally the troops.

"Baby, this is the first time I've felt confident in our chances since we started running."

Rosa looked at me like I'd been snorting snow.

"No, really," I said. "I know the going is getting tougher, but left to our own devices, I can get us out of here. My main worry has always been Cleeve and the boys. The compensation here is that the snow probably will be as hard on our enemies as it is on us, and only a maniac would take a helicopter out in weather like this."

"Cleeve *is* a maniac, Mac," she muttered.

"One with an appreciation of his own skin, though," I said. "And as long as this snow keeps up, it's going to be hard to snipe us from a distance. We've got a rifle now, albeit a pretty beat up one and it even has a scope."

"Look at the scope, too. This is excellent quality. It probably cost more than this ol' Marlin did brand new. What's up with that?"

"Same theory as before," I said. "I'll bet you five bucks and a donut that this rifle belongs to Three Feathers and the scope belongs to Cleeve. They find us dead in a valley with bullets from this rifle, which magically they find after the fact, without the scope. Three Feathers is made into the Mad Trapper of the Pasayten, murderer of the sheriff, the federal agent, and the two young trackers. Cleeve kills him, becomes the hero, takes over and case closed."

"Plan won't work if we make it out of here."

"Plan ain't gonna work, 'cause we *are* making it out of here."

                                        ****

I think rivers are things of beauty, but not in snow storms.

Not when I have to cross them.

"Do you see a good spot to wade across?" Rosa asked.

"Pretty deep down here. I think I see a beaver dam up above. Maybe we can use it as a bridge."

"I'd really, and I mean *really* like to not have to wade in that. It's going to be colder than Cleeve's heart," she said, looking at the emerald water, snowflakes disappearing into its surface.

"Take strength from this, if we have to wade. Nothing is as cold as Cleeve's heart."

"Thanks."

The beaver dam either was in the stage of final construction or repair. Both sides of the dam, had serious mud and stick construction looking very solid, but the center had only a latticework of downed logs with chewed sticks holding them in place. It was not sturdy enough to trust foot traffic on by any means.

"Look," I said, "the water level below the dam is fairly shallow. We can cross there, and I doubt it'll be higher than our waists."

Rosa gave me a look that indicated she was strongly considering shooting me.

"C'mon. I've got a trash bag in my butt pack," I told her. "Let's line that backpack with it and stuff all our gear and clothes in to protect them. Then, we wade."

"Our clothes!?"

"Better our bodies are wet for a short time, than our clothes are wet all day."

"Shit!"

"Shit, indeed."

"Mac, if this is your woodsy way of gettin' me outta my clothes, you've got a weird perversion going on here."

Rosa needn't have worried about my 'perversion.' The water was as unpleasantly cold as you might imagine, and though I admit seeing her beautiful bare body was having some effect on certain parts of my anatomy, when the water hit a spot below my waist all thoughts of romance were gone.

Far gone.

I've been in colder water, water so cold it hurts, but this small river was *plenty* cold enough. Stay in here for any considered length of time and hypothermia was assured. We moved quickly, using the base of the beaver dam for support.

"What I wouldn't give for a wetsuit right about n-n-n-ow," Rosa said from behind me.

"No kidding," I said, reaching out to steady myself in the belly deep water. I grabbed hold of a thick sapling sticking out of the front of the dam, and was mortified when it moved all too easily. There was creaking and groaning from the dam, and Rosa and I froze in position.

"*Madre de Dios*," Rosa said. "Was that what I think it was?"

"If you're thinking that, if that limb gets moved again," I said, taking a step back, "that we're likely to be carried downstream under a ton of water and debris, then yeah." I started moving toward the opposite bank as quickly as the current would let me. "That stick is the lynch pin of that entire section. Everything in that center section is tied to it."

"Ohshitohshitohshit!"

"Let's not discuss it, and get our little blue asses onto the opposite shore!"

We couldn't run in the waist deep water, but we did a pretty fair impression of it.

"Holy crap," Rosa said, rummaging through the pack for her clothes. "that was freaky."

"The beavers are still in the early stages on that section, putting logs and sticks in for a foundation. That foundation still needs a lot of work."

"Mac?" Rosa was shrugging into her pants when she noticed I was still standing in the falling snow in all my birthday-suited glory. "Why are you still naked?"

"Just realized something," I said, also realizing my chilly state. "Been looking for a good place for a trap and could this be any better?"

I pulled my pants out of the garbage bag, looked through the thigh pockets and pulled out a coil of paracord I keep there for emergencies. I cut about an eight-foot length, putting a slip knot loop on each end then, without putting my pants on, I grabbed my big knife and waded into the small river.

"Mac!" Rosa yelled. "Are you sure this is a good idea?"

"You'll see."

I'm not going to tell you that I liked being in the freezing water. In fact, I could feel myself starting to shiver uncontrollably, but this trap was going to be so simple I couldn't pass it up. I took a stick from the side of the beaver dam as I walked along and with a few strokes of my knife's sharp edge, I put a point on the end.

The next bit was not at all enjoyable. I dropped my head below the water, looking for just the right spot. Diving down, I jammed the stick into the sand and mud of the bottom and laying my knife over the end of the stick sideways, I used my fist to drive the stake in firmly. I then looped one end of the cord over it and pulled it tight. I rose up then, and very carefully tightened the other end, with its slip knot, over the lynch pin limb in the dam.

I didn't linger to admire my work.

Once back on shore, I put on my underwear and pants, trying to dry off with a bough from a nearby cedar as much as I could. I can't even express how wonderful it felt to put my shirt and jacket on. And boots. Boots and socks are such wonderful things.

"Think it'll work?" Rosa asked.

"If ol' Teeg's still on our trail, he'll probably cross here if we give him incentive." I pulled out an orange bandana I had seen in Holmes' pack. "Here we go."

I lay the bandana on the bank, putting part of it in the snowy grass so as not be too obvious.

"You think he'll cross here, instead of finding someplace else?"

"We looked up and down the creek. This was the best place to cross," I said. "We could've done a better job of hiding our tracks where we went across, but the snow's making it just hard enough, he'll have to work to stay with our trail. Suddenly, he sees a little flash of orange through the snowy grass. I can't see the future, but I think when Teeg sees that trace, it'll be like a pleasing lure to a trout."

Rosa looked at the river. "You know, I could probably just snipe him with this Marlin."

"You could, and if it comes to it you might have to. But at this point, we haven't put a bullet in anyone. I hate to sound Machiavellian, but as you said earlier, if we wind up in a trial somewhere and our enemies are injured by mishaps with nature, rather that direct action from us, it might be in our favor."

Rosa patted my cheek. "Ah, my naive *chiquito*, you've seen the lengths that Cleeve has gone to for framing Three Feathers. Do you really think he'd do any less for us? I think I'll wait here a bit to see if Mason stopped for Holmes. We can take a rest, dry our socks, and if he doesn't show up in an hour, we move on at the fastest pace we can."

"Agreed." Though I wondered if Rosa's real reason didn't have more to do with Teeg Mason and the rifle she carried.

****

It didn't take an hour.

We had pretty much dried out our clothes with our body heat and eaten snacks when Teeg Mason showed up on the other side of the little river, looking down at the faint trail of our passing. There was no way he could have stopped to help Holmes and been this close behind us. Rosa looked at me from the log we were hiding behind, the all-knowing eyebrow upraised.

Tough break, Holmes.

Through a screen of limbs, we watched Mason stop at the water's edge, and though I was too far to see his expression, his body language oozed with distaste at having to cross. He stood for a moment, and I knew from the way he raised up, he'd seen the bandana. Our tracks were somewhat obscured by snow, but the bright orange bandana made him stand tall, tense and excited. It seemed to spur him to a decision.

He stuffed his jacket in his daypack as well as his gloves and hat, then began to wade across, wearing the rest of his clothing and his boots. Rosa looked over at me, surprised at what she was seeing.

"He's gonna regret that if he survives." I whispered, "That's a great way to get hypothermia."

"I doubt he'll need to worry about it," Rosa said, a hard edge to her voice as she rechecked the safety on the rifle.

I've always had too big of an empathetic streak. When Mason hit the paracord, he was moving as quickly as he could, much as Rosa and I had been when we crossed earlier. Where I had merely touched the log that held the beaver dam puzzle together, he hit the paracord hard and it yanked on that log. Yanked strongly. My prediction of the effect was dead on.

The center section of the dam didn't all go, but Mason froze for a second as he realized how far in the deep and brown that he was in. With a creak, then a roar, part of the middle section gave way. Logs and sticks washed over him, propelled by a wall of cold water, and he disappeared, his pack and carbine flying from his hands. I became aware of the grimace on my face as his hands, the last part of him showing, disappeared beneath the water.

I looked at Rosa. She too had a sickened grimace on her face, but she only said, "Good trap."

That would have been the end of it, but then the largest log rolled, and for a moment, Teeg Mason clawed his way to the surface. He was trapped under the log, and it was slowly rolling and sending him back under. He was doomed and there was nothing he could do about it.

Teeg Mason saw us standing on the shore, watching him pathetically die, and he said just one word.

"Please!"

I'm not sure how it happened, but the next thing I remember, I was wading in thigh deep water moving to try and save him.

Yeah. Stupid.

Stupid, stupid, stupid.

I heard Rosa yell for me to come back. She was right, I was endangering myself, just to help someone who'd tried to kill me just because I couldn't stand to hear that word "please" and watch his terror as he died.

I was weak.

Weak! Weak! WEAK!

But I was still wading forward. I was about ten steps from the logjam when a vice-like grip grabbed the back of my collar and yanked me off my feet.

"Rosa!" I screamed. "Stop it! Goddam it, let me go!"

As I was dragged into the shallows, I twisted around to make her let go, and saw her standing on the bank a good ten feet away. She was looking behind me, an astonished expression on her face. I wound around to see who'd grabbed and dragged me back to shore.

I looked up into the weathered face of Jim Three Feathers.

"It's best you don't go over there, right now," he said.

I looked back towards Mason, who had managed to claw up high enough from under the log that he could raise a hand toward us, beseeching us to save him, terror on his face. Then, I heard the creaking and groaning from the beaver dam. Teeg had only been hit with the top layer of the dam, but now the entire middle of the structure began to slowly and unstoppably move down stream. With a roar, the whole thing finally gave way, and half a ton of sticks, mud, and water slammed down onto him.

I watched as the swollen mass crunched and ground its way along the river, and for a moment, I thought I saw one of Mason's legs in the rolling flotsam. Fifty yards downstream, the whole thing hit some large boulders and formed a logjam, everything mashed and grinding together.

Teeg Mason's tracking days were over.

CHAPTER TWENTY-TWO

"Nope. I'm not dead."

"We kinda noticed that, Mr. Three Feathers."

Jim Three Feathers looked to be about sixty years old, but it was hard to tell. He was fit as hell, with hands the size of catchers' mitts and a face that looked weathered enough that I guessed the majority of his life had been spent outdoors. His shoulder-length hair had a few gray strands, but it was mostly black. I hoped when I got to be this age, I had held up as well.

We were around a fairly good sized fire, built under a rocky overhang watching the snow pile up. Three Feathers was wiping down Teeg Mason's M-4 carbine that he'd manage to retrieve from the river. I sat in nothing but the camouflage poncho liner blanket, my steaming clothes sitting over logs to dry. Introductions had been brief.

"The question we have," Rosa said, "is how are you alive?"

He smiled. "Remember when ol' Cleeve shot me up there?"

"It's kinda hard to forget, Deputy Holmes shot me too. He just forgot I had a ballistic vest on."

Three Feathers mouth tightened. "Disgraceful men. Shooting a young girl."

"Evidently, I'm not the first, just the luckiest," she said.

"I was lucky too," Three Feathers told us. "That rifle Cleeve had was right outta my gun rack, just like that old Marlin there." He gestured to the rifle Rosa had been lovingly protecting from the snow and wet.

"We wondered why he was carrying that, and not some modern military style rifle," I said. "I'm guessing the shotgun was yours too?"

"Yep. They cleaned out my rack. Can't frame a fellow these days and use your own gun."

"So what happened on the hill?" Rosa asked, "I saw you get hit. I saw you slide down into the brush."

"Cleeve evidently didn't take my rifle out and practice with it much." He said, "It tends to pull down and to the left and I've just got so used to it, I compensate. Cleeve didn't. Knocked a chunk o' flesh off my right side." He pulled up his shirt and showed a bandage taped over his side. A small amount of blood leaked through.

"They missed you. They missed Rosa here."

"Guess they didn't miss that other fella wearin' the Forest Service uniform I found at the bottom of that cliff."

"That was Bill Farnsworth. I didn't know him long, but he was one of the good guys. That bastard Cleeve ambushed us by helicopter." I said, "Bill didn't have a chance."

"So were you tracking us?" Rosa said.

"Kinda. I was trackin' that young fella that was trackin' you."

"His name was Teeg Mason," I said, looking into the fire. "I set that trap at the beaver dam…"

"Looked like you was about to try an' fish him outta that mess."

"Yeah. Stupid, I guess."

"I respect that you was able to set that trap for him. I respect more that you was willing to try an' save him, but I could see it was a lost cause. That's why I went and grabbed you and dragged you back onto shore. What about that other guy? The one on the rockslide?"

We both looked up at him. "Holmes," Rosa said.

"He was going to snipe us from the top of that rockslide," I said. "Would have had us too if we… um.. hadn't been warned."

Rosa and I looked at each other. How do you explain something that sounds so much like something out of the Twilight Zone?

"Was Holmes still alive?" Rosa asked him.

"Just barely. He was covered by about six inches of snow and was on the way out, pretty much comatose. Looks like he had a bad fall. I've had run-ins with that ol' boy, as have many of the native peoples livin' in this area. Can't say I was overwhelmed with pity. He was your handiwork too?"

I admit I hesitated a moment before answering. "Yeah. We got into it with him, and I knocked him off those rocks."

"Didn't see no marks on him."

"It went hand to hand." I said, "I got lucky."

"Lucky!" Rosa laughed, "You kicked his sorry ass!"

"Well, I want you two youngsters to listen to what I have to say, and mind it." Three Feathers face was deadly serious. "As far as you're concerned, you never saw either o' those two men. All you know is that the deputies went crazy and killed the sheriff and that Farnsworth fella. You just been runnin' for your lives."

Rosa lifted up my jacket and showed him the tattered remain of her own, sitting over the scarred ballistic vest. "They tried to kill me," she said.

"Hang onto that stuff. You'll be glad you did. And when we get close to civilization, you take Mr. Holmes' pack and any gear of his that you might have and you deep six it into the nearest river with rocks inside."

"You want us to deny having seen them?"

"There are a lot of good cops in the world, son. They keep the modern world from sliding into crazed anarchy. But hidden in amongst them are those there for other reasons than protectin' and serving, unstable people who don't want justice, they want power." His face grew sour."I think Cleeve and his boys are one of them 'extreme examples' o' that. You got to be careful as a fox around them sort, 'cause they use the system like a personal weapon."

"Plausible deniability?" Rosa asked.

"Yeah," Three Feathers smiled, "I like that. Once we're out of here, Cleeve's gonna have to go into damage control and that means making you look like you're on the wrong side of the law. If he has you, then he can get you someplace to make you disappear."

"That can't work! The department called us up here! How the hell would he ever justify that?" I said.

"Lot of folks have been proven innocent after having been shot tryin' to escape." Three Feathers said, sighing, "Guns, drugs can be planted. Things a straight arrow cop wouldn't dream of doing. Those are the things a bad cop uses for an arsenal. Just let ol' Cleeve wonder what happened to his boys. Both of their deaths could be 'death by misadventure' as far as he knows."

"Give the enemy as little useful information as possible. Or misdirected info," Rosa said.

"Yep."

"And Cleeve's definitely the enemy," I said.

"I'd say so," Three Feathers replied. "Now, who warned you about deputy Holmes?"

****

It took less time than I thought to explain. Strange, strange coincidences with coyotes aren't the sort of thing you can discuss with your cubicle mates at the office without getting looks of concern for your mental wellbeing. Three Feathers, however, seemed to take the affair with a great deal of seriousness.

"Hmmm," he said. "You say it looked like the same track, and when you saw him, it looked like the same ol' boy with a scar on his side?"

"Yeah," I said, face turning a little red. "Kinda crazy, huh?"

"Most o' you white folks might think so, son. How long you been trackin'?"

"Since I was twelve. Just kinda developed a passion for it. It's like being a woodsy Sherlock Holmes." I said, "I can't describe how it makes me feel to be on a trail and staying with it…"

"You tracked me pretty good. Thought I was in the clear, then I see you and this little gal doggin' my heels and my tricks failin' me," he said. "I was kinda impressed."

It was only much later on that I would realize what a big thing it was to impress this man.

"If a person, man or woman, tracks long enough, spends enough time alone, their minds, I think even their brains, change. They become more open to certain… things, things most can't normally see," he continued, "I think you might be on a cusp there, Mac."

"What do you mean, Mr. Three Feathers?"

"Whyn't you call me Jim? If a person has the right mind set and concentrates his mind on things besides everyday reality, sometimes they see stuff, things most folks sort of unconsciously agree to *not* see. Old things. Things that have been here longer than this civilization by quite a bit. Maybe been here longer than we been walkin' on two legs."

"What sort of... things?" Rosa asked.

"Magic things. I can't be a hundred percent sure, but I think one of the oldest of those magic things may be taking an interest in Mac here." He turned from Rosa to me. "All you can do at this time, is keep your eyes open, son. Reality is often not always what it seems. It won't always fit in the little box modern man wants it to. But don't expect help all the time, neither. The old things don't coddle the weak, the unbelieving or the stupid."

"Supposing I do believe some of this," I said, "what am I supposed to do?"

"Like I said," he replied, "keep your eyes open for... interesting... occurrences. Don't let the chatter in your head take over all the time."

I found it improbable that this Native American mountain recluse was talking to me about the same things that a Buddhist monk would. But truth be told, it was pretty far down on the list of unbelievable things that had happened to me this week.

"Someday, down the road a ways, and assuming we're all still alive," Three Feathers said, "you make your way up here to see me. I feel I got a responsibility to you here, and I think you'll have one to me."

"When?"

He laughed. "When your brain ain't able to wrap around it anymore. That'll be the time. Now, we have more immediate things we need to discuss."

"Like how to get our asses of here," Rosa said.

"Heh, yeah. I reckon so," Three Feathers said. "Either of you two got one of them cell phones? Wait. What am I sayin'... you're both under forty, you were probably each born with one in your hand."

"I do," Rosa admitted, "but the battery is just about dead. Mac? You've kept yours turned off. Check it to see how much you've got left."

"Sure," I said, reaching for my pants. As soon as I touched the wet fabric, I had a sinking feeling in my stomach. "Oh... shit."

"You didn't."

I pulled my cell out of the thigh pocket I'd stuffed it when I turned it off. I'd been carrying it in the butt pack, but had just stuffed it in my pocket last time I'd checked it trying to keep it warm. I hit the power button and waited.

And waited.

Nothing.

"Oh damn," I said.

"You didn't!" I could see Rosa's steam rising.

"Uh... yeah. It was in my pants when I went in after Teeg. It's not powering up."

"Oh dammit, Mac! Now our job just got a lot harder. We're gonna have to find someone with a phone, not just find a signal now."

"Yeah. I definitely screwed up. I just... when I saw his face... I just..." I couldn't finish. I couldn't even explain it rationally. Teeg Mason had been part of a team trying to kill us, yet when I'd seen that pleading horror on his face, I'd acted without thinking. I was pretty sure none of my military-trained friends would have done something so dumb.

"You care for this young man?" Three Feathers said to Rosa.

"I..." I was surprised to see her blush, "Yes. Yes, I do... a lot."

"Then just be glad you found a man with a good heart. It's hard to be a warrior and still have compassion for your enemies. From everything I've seen of the two of you, you both have warrior hearts."

Rosa is not one for embarrassment. She's usually the one taking the world head-on and damn the torpedoes. This time, she turned even a bit more red under her cinnamon skin.

"I... yeah. Sorry, Mac."

"Don't be. It would have taken me only a second to have tossed my phone to you before I waded in there. Can't call *that* mindfulness."

"As I was sayin'," Three Feathers cut in, "I know the best way to get out of here. Hiking out through this snowstorm isn't gonna be easy, but it won't kill us. Best exit point is Green Creek campground, though this snow probably has driven the last of the hardcore campers back home by now. At least it's a road to 'out there' where you can find a phone."

"Is it gonna do us much good to be at a snow-filled campground?" I asked. "If I know the forest service, they've probably locked up the bathrooms already for the year and it's getting towards evening.

I don't want to try to tramp out of there in the dark."

"Well, here's where you might not be as enthused with the plan. Before you get there, I'm gonna part ways with you both."

"What?"

"If you two happen to show up, Cleeve can't just start shooting at you, out there in front of the whole world. He may detain you, but it's gonna look damn strange even at that, since lots of folks know you were hired by the sheriff. If I show my face, there's a good chance I'll be shot 'resisting arrest' by the acting sheriff."

"Surely he'd have to be more discreet than that," Rosa said.

"Ol' Cleeve has laid a lot of groundwork by now sayin' I killed that girl and that's probably enough for most people to say to themselves "Oh, he musta had it comin,' him being a murder an' all." Three Feather's face grew grim, "Most folks want an easy answer. They don't want to think too much about things and if an easy answer comes their way, they'll grab it and hang on to it unless overwhelming evidence says otherwise. Hell, some will hold on to their first opinion in even in the face of overwhelming evidence. Thinking and changin' their minds is just too hard."

"Why's he doing all this? It can't be only to be sheriff again." Rosa said.

"My cousin Lincoln had me nosin' around a little, He had an idea that Cleeve was somehow involved with the meth 'tweakers' around here. I think I was startin' to find out some stuff the former sheriff didn't want uncovered, and probably right around then, he decided to frame me."

"If he's that good at it, I bet he's been laying some groundwork about Rosa and me too, then." I said.

"Yeah," Three Feathers continued, "but there are stories to keep straight here. I'd guess Dominic Cleeve right now is wondering what the hell happened to his boys. I'm thinking the original story was to have you two, the sheriff, and that Forest Service fella dead by my hands. Is it time to change you two from victims into bad guys? Gotta come up with a plausible story there."

"Whatever he comes up with, it's gonna be a lie," Rosa said.

"Maybe so," Three Feathers said, an edge of bitterness to his voice, "But lie or truth, all he has to do is sell it."

CHAPTER TWENTY-THREE

Hiking in a snow storm can be one of the most beautiful experiences a person will ever have. Or, conversely, it can be one of the circles of Hell. The snow was up to the top of my calves and over Rosa's knees. It was wet going.

Three Feathers had a little deer jerky, and we had our remaining two Holmes-provided energy bars before we'd set out, but I think all of us were flagging a bit from the hunger. The average person uses about 2500 calories a day, but we had to be burning through twice that easily. We sure weren't taking in that many.

Three Feathers and I had been taking turns breaking trail, though Rosa had insisted on doing her part early on. Our longer legs made it easier for us and she eventually decided to stop worrying about sexism and let us take point without argument. We were all glad when the older man pointed at the base of a big pine where the snow hadn't been able to reach and signaled a halt.

"I will never again take these big pine trees for granted," Rosa said.

"It's sure nice to have some dry pine needles to sit on. My pant legs are soaked," I told her.

"Yeah. Mine too."

"Old Man Pine provides," Three Feathers said. "Can't tell you the number of times my only blanket has been a bunch a these pine needles."

"I don't think I've ever been this tired," I said. Rosa and I were sitting back to back, leaning against each other and energy levels were low.

"Ha!" Three Feathers said, "You ain't never been hungry if this is takin' it outta you."

Rosa turned to him, and said quietly, "I've been hungry. Real hungry." I watched over my shoulder the look the two of them exchanged. Three Feathers looked away first.

"I guess you have," he said.

There was so much about Rosa I didn't know at all. She didn't often say much about her past before the marines.

"I had a brother and two sisters," she said. "My mom often forgot to feed us, or spent all the money she got from assistance to feed her habit. Half of what we ate was what I could beg, borrow, or steal."

"I... didn't know any of that, Rosa," I said.

"There's a lot you don't know about me, Mac," she said. "Maybe you might want to be more careful who you hook up with."

"I have been. I know who you are now, and I'm proud to be with you."

"Mac..." she stopped and looked away. But her hand crept into mine. "Someday I'll tell you... what I can bear to."

"Can't say fairer than that."

"Ah, so..." Three Feathers, uncomfortable at our private moment, interrupted, "The trail that leads to the campground is coming up. I think it'd be best I took my rifle, and if you folks only had what you carried into the mountains on you. Give me Holmes' pack and gear and I'll make sure it's never found again."

It was strange to me, us sitting there, deciding on the truth we would present. But in his way, Three Feathers echoed things my Uncle Gil always said. In a court of law, the truth was subjective, and it was best to make the truth shine in your favor whenever possible. Bounty hunters were always in danger of being sued, or having a police officer give us trouble, even if we were legally within our rights.

Bottom line: best to be careful and meticulous.

"Where will you go, Mr. Three Feathers?" Rosa asked.

"Jim. From now on, call me Jim," he said. "I'm gonna make contact with some tribal members I know that have no love for Dominic Cleeve and go to ground. He'll have to have come up with quite a yarn to try and sell, not only to the law around here, but also the feds and surviving family members. The whole thing depends on all of us bein' dead."

"I'd prefer to avoid that part," I said. "I'm glad we still have my Glock, just in case."

"Here's what I suggest. If we split up here, we have twice as much chance of at least one of us gettin' the word to people who can do something about this. When you two hit the campground, if there's no one there, it's about ten miles to the highway. Flag down a passerby, and get out of Loman County. Once you've passed from Cleeve's jurisdiction, you get to a phone and start callin' for help. You both seem pretty savvy, and I'm guessin' you know people who know people."

"We work for a bounty hunter, my uncle Gil. He has friends at the local office of the FBI as well as Chelan County Sheriff's department. I think we have that covered."

"Then may the Old Ones watch over you." Three Feathers said, "See you later."

Jim Three Feathers stepped into the snowstorm, and in ten steps he was gone.

****

Murphy's Law, of course, dictated that the campground had to be completely empty.

Setbacks like this, when you're hungry and tired, take the spark out of you, but they also show your mettle. My stomach, as the old saying goes, 'felt like my throat must've been cut' and the hunger gnawed at me. I wasn't going to show a crap attitude to Rosa though, no matter how low my blood sugar was. I could see she was dog tired and probably hungry as a bear too, but there was nary a complaint.

"Cheeseburger," I said.

"Oh, are we really doing this?" she said, rolling her eyes at me.

"When we get to someplace safe, it's gonna be a double cheeseburger, large fries, and of course, the prerequisite banana milkshake."

"Banana, feh," Rosa replied, contemptuous of such an exotic option, "Strawberry is known to be the milkshake of choice for truly tough bounty hunters." In her best Schwarzenegger impression she informed me, "Banana is for da gully mens."

"I find myself astonished at this information you're imparting."

She sniffed. "I'm appalled at your lack of education in the matter."

"Well, oh Swami, what are you going to eat on our arrival at some poor unsuspecting restaurant?"

"Surf and turf, my Padawan. Lobster and steak, big ol' baked potato and a salad with ranch. A good old fashioned 'Murican dinner."

"What?" I asked, "What about the carné asada? What about the enchiladas, tacos, and the churros of your people."

"Thank you Mister Stereotype," she said, "Perhaps you should have some haggis at the next Irish restaurant we come to?"

"Well, since in our humble little town," I said, "there's only one Irish tavern and thirty-five Mexican restaurants, I thought you might like to carb up…"

"Honestly," she said. "I'm so hungry that even your skinny white butt is starting to look less like a source of carnal joy, and more like a quick snack."

"Hoo, boy. Donner Party here we come."

****

We managed to keep each other's spirits up for the first six miles or so, but eventually, the slog through knee-deep snow turned into a wintery version of the Battan Death March.

By the time Rosa and I were almost to the two-lane highway, we were having trouble staying warm, having burned through all our bodily fuel. Just as we came to the plowed highway, a pickup pulled into the campground road and a shaggy head leaned out of the driver window.

"You two look like you need a lift!" Our benefactor had lank hair sticking out of a beat up old John Deere baseball cap that just touched the shoulders of a well-used Carhart barn coat. His face, though not old, looked like it had seen its miles of bad road and his long teeth and receding gum indicated dental care didn't seem to be something he was acquainted with. His truck however, was impressive. As one whose form of transportation could be most charitably categorized as a 'rattle trap,' the brand new Toyota Tundra pickup was more than a little envy inducing.

"Hi, my name's Joe," I said, "this is Chloe..." I had noticed that Rosa giving me an arched eyebrow as she jerked her eyes toward the driver. "We...ah.. kinda got lost hiking, and then this snowstorm moved in. We'd sure appreciate a ride."

"M'name's Herman," he said. "You two just hop on in. I'll crank the heater up and getcha someplace nice. Hell of a time to be on foot!"

We dusted the snow off our clothes as best we could. Rosa entered first, taking the center section of the bench seat while I pulled off my butt pack and harness. I climbed in and set it on the floor between my feet.

Herman opened his door, taking the keys. "Hey, um... gimme a second wouldja? I been in this rig a while and I really need to take a little trip into the woods over there. Hope you don't mind." He grabbed a roll of toilet paper from under the seat and headed out into the thick forest, leaving a trail in the fallen snow.

"Well, what do you think of Herman?" I asked.

"Beggars can't be choosers, but.. there's an odd smell to him, not cigarettes, but..." Rosa replied "Can't quite think what it is, but I know he doesn't bathe too often. Or do laundry."

"You want the window seat?"

"No, I'm all right. If we can just get out of this county, or even to a payphone, I'll be very happy," Rosa said. "And if Herman can get us there, he wears angel wings in my book."

We waited almost ten minutes, then he came wading through the snow out of the trees. The flakes were falling even harder than they had been earlier, and he looked like he was part yeti.

"Sorry that took so long," he said. "You gotta go, but when you get to where you can go, suddenly everything's kinda clogged up."

"No worries," I said, doing my best to keep visuals of his words out of my mind. "Are you heading any direction in particular?"

"Headin' towards McClellan. Ain't much else out here to go to, if you get my meaning."

"Y'know, if you could just get us someplace close to there with a payphone, we could call friends who could come and pick us up, help us get back to our truck before it's snowed in for the winter."

"Hey, man, I know just the place." Herman's scraggly teeth

erupted in a smile. "There's a state rest stop with bathrooms, a payphone, and even some vending machines. There's even covered walkways to keep the snow off. 'Fraid the local Lions Club has shut down their coffee sellin' operation for the year though."

"That would be great. We've been foodless for a while, and right now, vending machines sound like a little piece of heaven," Rosa said.

"Shoot. I had some donuts, but I ate 'em before I found you two," Herman said, sounding regretful over the heart-rending news. "Sorry."

"It's okay," I said, trying to put a good face on the tragedy. "We'll have our friends pick some up on the way when they come to get us."

"I wonder if there's an outlet there somewhere that I can charge my phone," Rosa asked. "We can call collect from a payphone if we need to, but I'd like to have a working phone on me."

"Cell reception is pretty bad up in these parts." Herman told her, "Damn big phone companies don't think enough people live out this way to make it worth their while. Same with all them big box stores. You wanna go to a Walmart, man, you gotta go all the way to Omak, a dang hour drive."

As we cruised on through the semi-blizzard, Herman vented to us his feelings on all the shortcomings of living in such a remote county. He'd been born and raised here, and to his way of thinking had never caught a break, a claim that seemed at odds with the fine truck we were riding in.

I internally sighed. He wasn't the first person I'd met who lived in a very beautiful place, but could only see the disadvantages. Not to make myself seem smart, but I thanked the Creator for every day I was able to spend living in my dinky little Airstream along the Columbia River.

To break up the kvetch fest, I asked, "So, Herman, what do you do around here. Construction? Logging? Farmer?"

"I...ah..." His eyes turned back to the road. "I hurt my back a few years ago doin' handyman stuff. I get terrible pain if I get too physical, ya know what I'm sayin'?"

"Oh? Tough break man." I said, "You get a settlement or something?"

"Naw, but I got disability. Helps keep the lights on, y'know?"

"Ah," I said, "Well, that's good." He'd seemed pretty spry when he was climbing over snow-laden logs to go out for his bathroom break in the forest, but it wasn't any of my business.

"You two married?" he asked. Rosa looked at me, blushing slightly.

Herman noted the blush. "Haw! Maybe not, but looks like someone's been thinkin' about it!"

She didn't reply, but her warrior princess's blush only deepened.

Somehow, I liked that. A lot.

"Who knows," Rosa finally said. "We're still figuring things out."

"I was married for a while," Herman said.

The next several mile were taken up with Herman reporting to us what a bitch his ex-wife had been, how she hadn't understood him, and left him when he was down. The droning of his slightly nasal voice began to lull me to sleep, and the days of running and the soft seats of the Toyota didn't help.

I awoke when Rosa nudged me, having no idea how much actual time had passed. It still looked like early afternoon as we pulled into the rest stop. The snow was coming down hard still, and it looked like the snowplows placed a low priority on cleaning out the rest stop. A good eight inches had fallen on the parking lot since it had last been plowed, and the single set of tire tracks told me only one car had been brave enough to enter before us. Most sensible people were very likely at home watching TV or reading a book.

"Lights are on," I said. "At least they haven't shuttered the place."

"Thank God," Rosa said. "If those bathrooms are locked, I'm going to be a very unhappy camper."

We exited the truck, and tramped through the deepening snow and were rewarded with bathrooms not only unlocked, but heated. It was a luxury after several days of doing business in the woods. Rosa and I emerged from opposite bathrooms almost at the same time.

"Hey," I said. "Where's Herman?"

"Truck's gone."

"Was it something we said?"

"Guess he decided to not stick around." Rosa said, "Look. Pay phone. Let's call the cavalry." She began walking over to a row of pay phones, and I looked at where Herman's truck had been sitting. The tracks moved off and around the facility, probably looping the place then returning to the exit on the other side of the rest stop. I crossed the covered walkway past the bathroom on a whim, seeing if I could see his tire tracks on their exit path.

No tracks going out.

What the hell? Did he back the truck out?

It was then that I saw Herman's ride sitting against the back fence. There was another vehicle beside it, difficult to make out through the gloom and the falling snow. I started to wander out that way to get a closer look.

"Mac!" Rosa's voice called out, panic in her tone.

I ran back to where I had left her, wishing I had the .45 pistol that I gave her earlier. As I came around the corner, I saw her standing there, hands on her head, fingers laced together.

Behind her, Herman stood, grinning, with an AR-15 pointed at the back of her head.

Oh shit. He's a damn serial killer.

Then I felt something cold touch the back of my neck. Looking over my shoulder and down the barrel of an old rifle, I saw the smiling face of Dominic Cleeve.

CHAPTER TWENTY-FOUR

We were on our knees, hands zip-tied behind us. Herman held his weapon loosely, but aimed in our general direction. Cleeve had walked over to the pay phones and was making a call.

"Guess you had us fooled, Herman," Rosa said.

"Well o'course, darlin,' that ain't no surprise." He gave us the long toothed smile. His receding gum line made it even more creepy than it had originally seemed. "You all just looked at the surface of ol' Mr. Hillbilly. Poor folks always help out strangers, and rich folks just pass by, right? Ain't that the liberal way of viewin' things?" His voice quieted as if telling a huge secret, "Well, actually, I'm a lot richer than you might think."

"And a lot sneakier," I said.

"Well, you know, 'country boy can survive' an' all that."

"I'm guessing you work for Cleeve," Rosa said. "Making meth? I noticed that slight chemical smell on you, under the cigarette smoke. Couldn't quite place it, but that's what it is, isn't it?"

Herman got a cagey look in his eyes, not well concealed.

"I just do odd jobs when the deputies is overwhelmed," he said, looking away from us. "He called me 'n a couple others, and said to cruise the trailheads, lookin' for a pair o' fugitives. I'm proud to do my civic duty." He said it as if also proud of coming up with a viable lie.

"C'mon, Herman," I said. "You know as well as I do that Cleeve wants us dead so he can cover up his murdering the sheriff."

Herman looked away again. "Don't know nuthin' 'bout that. Cleeve's got a couple of feds comin' to collect you two fer questioning in the death of that Forest Service guy. He says you shot that poor dude, shot him off a cliff."

Herman's body language told me he was lying through his teeth, but I still wondered why Rosa and I weren't dead yet. I couldn't imagine why Cleeve wouldn't have shot us on sight, and I highly doubted there were feds coming to take us in for questioning. I was fairly certain if that happened, we would be able to, if not convince them, certainly be able to cast a great deal of doubt on Cleeve's version of events.

"I'm guessing Cleeve probably has a gang of some sort. Takes more than three people to run a drug smuggling ring," Rosa said. "If I'm gonna guess, I'd say you and at least whoever was flying that logging helicopter Cleeve was in when he committed murder. Probably more people than that."

"Don't know nuthin' about yer wild speculations," Herman told her.

"That's right, he doesn't," Cleeve said as he walked up. He looked pointedly at Herman, who looked away. "So, I'm asking you now as acting sheriff of Loman County, where are my two deputies, Mason and Holmes?"

"No idea," Rosa told him. "Last time we saw them, you and they were trying very hard to murder us."

"Really. I seem to have lost contact with my boys. You sure you don't know anything about that?"

"Those mountains, this snowstorm. Maybe your boys weren't prepared for this and the Pasayten ate 'em," I said.

"Maybe, but I doubt it," Cleeve said. "Maybe that'll be something else for you two to answer for when the FBI takes you into custody. I've got some evidence that links you with Three Feathers, and implicates you in the murder of sheriff Dave Belshaw."

"Oh come *on*!" Rosa said, "We saw you shoot the sheriff in the head! You shot Three Feathers without so much as a warning! You blew poor Bill Farnsworth off that cliff face, goddam it! You can't believe you're going to get away with a story that thin! Any evidence you have is totally manufactured."

"As long as it's sellable, honey, that's all we need."

****

Cleeve drove us into town, to the sheriff's office parking lot. The snow had finally stopped falling for a while, and a black van marked 'FBI' pulled into the lot. Cleeve left us alone in the patrol car with Herman.

"I can't believe he's going to try to sell this to the FBI," I said.

"He's a hell of a planner," Rosa said, conscious of our hillbilly 'savior' in the front seat. "Seems he's been one step ahead of us the entire time. He might actually have a lie that convincing. I'm sure he's an expert at manufacturing evidence."

"You two ain't got no idea who you been workin' against," Herman said, turning back to us from the passenger seat. "Ol' Cleeve is three steps ahead of everyone. Makes me glad I'm on his team."

"Yeah," I said. "The team that when a plan goes south just tries to murder and lie their way out."

Herman lost his grin and turned back to the front, head aimed towards the office. Looking past him, I could see Cleeve and deputy Lincoln Davies arguing strongly, stopping only when the two dark-suited FBI agents stepped up to speak to them.

"You think Davies is in on this?" I asked Rosa quietly, but not quietly enough.

"Fuckin' injun," Herman said, contempt dripping from his words. "They all cause more problems around here than any ten white folks. Ol' Davies been a thorn in my ass. He'll get what's comin' eventually."

Thanks, Herman, for that info.

I glanced at Rosa and a knowing look passed between us. This was the first bit of good luck and solid information we'd had since the truck stop. You've got to use what little you can get.

"Don't like the native folks much, Herman?" I asked.

"Them and their confederated tribes," Herman's voice was filled with the hate only a dedicated racist could muster, the kind of hate that needs a scapegoat for its owner's shortcomings. "Go to their damn casinos, and they cheat the hell out of a man. Thinkin' they're such hot shit. No injun should be better off than a white man."

The hot reply I was about to give was interrupted when Rosa nudged me and pointed out the windshield with her chin. I looked up and saw that Cleeve walking our way, accompanied by the agents. He opened the door on Rosa's side and gestured for us to get out.

"Watch your heads," he said, perfunctorily. "This is Agent Smith and Agent Flynn. They'll be taking you two to the FBI office in Spokane."

Smith was a big man in a black suit, with a black tie, his eyes were close set, almost ape-like. The look he gave Rosa and I was as warm as the look that dedicated gardeners gave to aphids. Flynn was fairly small in comparison, close-cropped hair, prematurely balding, and he grinned as if at a joke none of the rest of us knew.

I started to take a breath in, to protest the entire situations, when I noted the look Rosa gave me. Ever so imperceptibly she shook her head.

Message received, wait 'til we're away from Cleeve to talk to the agents.

We were led to the back of the black panel van by the bulky Agent Smith, and I expected that our zip-ties would be replaced with handcuffs, but I was mistaken. We were rather unceremoniously seated on benches running down the side of the van. Smith sat across from us, and Flynn went forward to drive.

We had barely left the parking lot when we began to plead our case to the dour agent.

"We didn't shoot anyone!" I led out. "Rosa and I were hired by the sheriff's department. We've never even been to this area before!"

"Cleeve took us all out in the mountains," Rosa continued, "to find Three Feathers, then he and his cronies planned to kill us all, including the sheriff so he could take the county over again! Look at my coat! They shot me with a shotgun."

"You're doing awfully well for someone who's been shot," Smith said.

"I was wearing a vest," she said.

"Yeah, we've got your gear," the agent started to say.

"And Cleeve shot Bill Farnsworth," I interrupted. "Shot him from some lumber company helicopter. The pilot must've been part of his team."

"We think Cleeve's got some sort of meth making operation up here, and that's why he got rid of Sheriff Belshaw…"

Smith raised his big blunt hands. "Just… shut it for a moment. I don't know about any of this, but we got the sheriff of this little piss ant county who has informed us that you two are implicated in the murder of a federal officer. An officer, I might add, whose body hasn't been recovered in this snow storm..."

"Which," Agent Flynn's voice came from up front, "looks like it's starting up again."

"Great," Smith continued. "Anyway, we're all going to Spokane, where our investigators will be happy to listen to your whole story. The sheriff told our office that you were involved. Frankly, we're a lot more likely to take the word of a law officer over the word of two young punks who're trying to save their own posteriors. So both of you, just sit, relax, and we'll make this stupidly long van ride go as quickly as possible."

"Do we get a phone call?" I asked.

"Spokane."

At this moment, I began to wonder if Cleeve actually was going to be able to frame us. Our alibi was that we'd been hired to help the sheriffs and had never been in McClellan before. What kind of lies had the *de facto* sheriff manufactured? It seemed crazy that he could even remotely get away with something like this, but all he really needed was some sort of evidence that we'd been up here before and involved with questionable people.

Rosa and I looked at each other, she just shook her head in disbelief and looked at the floor.

"Could be worse," I told her, loud enough that our FBI watchdog could hear, "Cleeve could have just murdered us at that rest stop and buried our bodies out in the woods."

"Like he's murdered just about everyone else that went out there," she said.

"Cleeve said two of his deputies were missing," Smith said, "Know anything about that?"

"They were hunting us out in the wilderness," I said, remembering Three Feathers' earlier words, "I'd guess they're probably lost out there somewhere in the snow."

Not precisely a lie.

****

We were somewhere in Washington State east of the Cascade Mountains, that's all I knew.

There are roads in eastern Washington that lead through miles and miles of sagebrush country, interspersed with farmland, and some of them don't look like they get a whole hell of a lot of traffic. We'd been driving, at my best estimate, not more than an hour, but it felt like five. Occasionally I saw headlights through the falling snow, far away out the back window, but they would soon disappear. I doubted anyone wanted to stay on this particular throughway very long. The only snow removal was the powder being blown off the asphalt by our passing.

Rosa's head was leaning against my shoulder, and for all intents and purposes, she looked asleep. Smith also was starting to doze off, which I thought was pretty damn unprofessional for a law officer with two prisoners sitting across from him. His eyes kept drifting slowly closed and then would open with a jerk when we'd hit a big flaw in the road. This particular road gave his eyes a workout.

Smith's chin had just started a slow downward trajectory toward his chest when I heard a breathy whisper in my ear. "His shoes."

Rosa's eyes appeared to be closed, but I could see a glitter between her long lashes. She was wide awake. I very casually let my own head drop just enough to look at the agent's footwear and what I saw took a moment to register. Generally, the law enforcement agencies of the federal government have certain dress code standards when not undercover, and I was pretty sure Agent Smith's size fourteens were not in compliance. Aside from the fact they were scuffed and unshined, they were a dark brown against dark charcoal gray slacks. Upon closer inspection, I saw the slacks didn't quite match the black suit jacket either.

I began to get a bad feeling.

I'm a tracker. I'm supposed to be noticing crap like this with a Holmesian ability, but often when I'm out of the woods, that's not the case. Add to that Rosa and I hadn't had any food since the few snacks with Three Feathers and had been dragging our tails through the snow for a few days and my awareness seemed to have gone to sleep.

Well, it was awake now.

Smith's pants seemed to fit him fairly well, though the beginning of a paunch was starting to spill over his belt. His jacket, though unbuttoned, looked a half size too small and his thick wrists extended too far out of the sleeves.

Maybe he was just the sloppiest field agent ever. Maybe the laundry shrunk his jacket, and he had a tough time finding comfy clodhoppers for those big feet?

His suit coat slid back a little, and I saw the butt of the pistol he carried in a shoulder holster under his left arm. My gut clenched. It was a Ruger pistol, a .22 LR semi-automatic, not the standard Model 1911 or Glock 23 that FBI agents carried.

A .22 made a good gun for assassinations, killings at close range where you wanted minimum mess. No federal agent carried such a small caliber weapon, other than as a possible backup, and a backup wouldn't be in the primary access holster under his arm. There might have been another, larger caliber pistol on his belt, maybe over the base of his spine, I couldn't tell. But this .22 was in the spot that made it the go-to gun.

FBI agents my ass. Cleeve was 'disappearing' us.

CHAPTER TWENTY-FIVE

"All right, boys and girls. Pit stop." Flynn's voice came from the front of the van. The road for the last ten minutes had been especially bumpy, and I was hoping I was not going to see what I saw when Smith opened the back doors.

Nothing.

I had hoped we were stopping at an actual Department of Transportation rest stop, but from what I could see through the storm, and from the tracks our van had left, it was a remote dirt parking lot of some kind. There were no cars in the snowy lot. It was completely deserted, probably until the spring thaw.

"Where are we goin' to go to the bathroom?" Rosa asked.

Smith pointed to a small pair of metal building at the far end of the lot.

"We couldn't have parked down there?" I asked.

"Flynn's nervous about getting stuck."

I looked around, and through the snow I could see we were in about as empty a place as you could find. Most likely a trailhead to a fishing spot, the surrounding area looked like nothing but sagebrush and old lava rock cliffs. A perfect location, if one was willing to move some rocks around, to hide a body or two for a very long time.

Rosa and I hadn't let on that we knew something was up. We had very little going in our favor at the moment, and any opportunity to surprise our captors was not to be thrown away. If they were going to let us go into the primitive restrooms alone, I might be able to get rid of the zip ties binding my wrists.

Then I'd only have to face two killers, both armed with guns. Easy peasy.

"Um... how are we supposed to go, with our hands zip-tied behind our backs?" Rosa asked.

"You know what they say, necessity is the mother of invention," Flynn said, smirking.

Rosa went into the small metal outhouse on the left, and looking back at our captors, I went in the one on the right. The second the door was closed, I was kneeling on the less-than-sterile floor and rummaging in the sock of my right boot, and was immensely relieved to feel the tiny lock-blade knife I kept there. Unlike the last time I had to do this (not my first time being zip-tied) I was able to get my hand on it and pull it out without a problem. I snapped open the tiny one-inch serrated blade and awkwardly sawed at the plastic strip wrapped around my wrists. The tiny teeth on the blade worked their miracle, and my hands were free.

What now, Superman?

I had no idea how I was going to pull this off, but I wasn't going to have long to think of a plan. The metal shed/outhouse might be able to stop a .22 round, but I doubted that was the only hardware they were carrying. Any larger size caliber would probably go right through the walls, if not the door. Locking ourselves in wasn't really an option.

There were small holes in the metal door, which I realized were old bullet holes. For a moment I thought the plan was to take us out here and shoot the bathrooms we were in until blood flowed out under the door. Then I realized the holes were random, most likely made by the local lack-witted vandals who had shot up most of the signage in places like this. I hadn't noticed them on the way in with all the snow falling, and evidently, the boys hadn't really noticed either. I could hear them talking quietly.

"Honestly, Joseph," Flynns voice muttered quietly, "Why let them go to the bathroom? Let's just do this."

"These are young people, Arnold. From what I gathered, maybe young lovers. I just wanted to give them the option of not having their pants filled with shit when we end their sad little lives," Smith said.

"Oh Jesus, you're taking this whole 'gentleman assassin' thing way too far. It ain't professional."

I knew all I needed to know. I looked around the almost dark enclosure, and the only things there were a half-roll of toilet paper and a tupperware container on the floor holding a full roll. Not really what you'd want to storm the battlements with.

"Okay," a voice called out, "you've been in there long enough. Come out, right now!"

There was one other item that I had overlooked. I kicked the lid of the toilet seat, and with my adrenaline rushing, it snapped at the hinges and rattled on the floor.

"What the hell are you doing in there? Flynn, warning shot."

A huge sound came from outside and a hole appeared in the top of the outhouse, and it was a much bigger hole than a .22 would make. They could fill this little shelter with lead if they wanted to.

"Holy shit!" I yelled, "Just gimme a chance to get my flippin' pants back up! Hands tied, remember?"

"Hurry it up!"

The voice sounded like they were right in front of the door, just a ways out. I decided I would just slam open the front door and fling the seat discus style at one and try to do a Chuck Norris on the other, taking his gun.

Admittedly, in the history of shitty plans, this was a high ranker.

"Are you coming out?"

"What?" I yelled. "I can't hear you through the door!"

"Come the fuck out of there!" The voice was much closer, seemingly right outside the door. It was now or never.

I violently threw open the door, and about fifteen feet in front of me, Flynn stood holding a pistol almost as big as the van he'd been driving. I had the toilet seat ready to throw and was just starting to send it it at his head when lightning stuck me in the arm.

I've been tazed once before, and that time, the sadistic bastard had held the Taser against me for several eternal seconds. This time, the electrocution was much more brief, but I still wound up with my face sliding through the snow and my limbs uncontrollably spasming.

Smith stepped into my vision from where he'd stood at the side of the outhouse and looked down at me, shaking his head.

"Good effort, kiddo. Ain't my first rodeo, but points for trying," He said. Turning to the other outhouse, he yelled, "All right, missie. Yer boy here is convulsing on the ground. You can stay there for a while if you want, but I think it'd be best if you came out to help him."

Through my pain, I heard the door swing open, and Rosa's voice called out, "Mac! Oh Jesus! What'd you do to him!?"

"He got cute, he got Tasered. Simple math," Flynn sneered, aiming the huge pistol at her. "Help him to his feet. We're gonna take a little walk."

"So you can execute us?" she asked, ice in her voice.

The both looked a little surprised. "So, you figured it out?" Smith asked.

"No FBI agent would look as sloppy as you, unless undercover," She answered. "Cleeve hired you to finish us off someplace nice and lonely."

"Smart, smart girl," Smith said, sighing. "In a world with so many stupid people, it's gonna be a shame to remove you two from the gene pool. Almost an insult to Mr. Darwin. Nonetheless, when you got a job to do, you got to do it well."

"You got to give the other fella hell!" Flynn shouted. Both grinned at their little joke. "Get him to his feet! We'll do it up outta sight in that little aroyo over there. No one'll probably find 'em for years, the trail to the lake goes the other direction."

"For fuck's sake, Flynn. How's she gonna do that? Her hands are still tied. Gimme the hand cannon, and cut that zip-tie with yer flippy knife."

"You sure? I'm not happy with both these two being untied."

"If the young lady gets cute, the young man here will take a round from your Desert Eagle right in the temple," Smith said. "Do we understand each other?"

I couldn't see if Rosa nodded, but I watched Flynn pull a Filipino Balisong knife from his hip pocket, and of course he did all the cinematic whipping of the handles to open it. He reached behind Rosa while Smith aimed the large pistol at my head. In a second she was free and trying to help me to my feet.

"Rosa, I don't... I can't..." I couldn't finish.

"I know, Mac." She said, sadness in her voice, "We lost. Cleeve won."

****

We didn't have to walk too far through the falling snow. Our captors were wearing dress shoes, even if they were poorly maintained, and the shoes had smooth bottoms. For a moment, watching Flynn slip for the third time, I thought we might get away if we could just get a head start.

It wasn't to be. We were barely out of sight of the parking lot when Smith called a halt.

"I think this will do. No one will find them here 'til spring, and by then any 'dainty' evidence will have been destroyed by the snow."

"Should have just got to this, first thing," Flynn grumped. "don't know why you had to let 'em go to the bathroom."

"We've been through this. They're young people, Flynn," Smith said, with a long suffering air. "A quick shot with the .22 and voila, pretty corpses."

"They're not going to give a flying fuck! They'll be dead!"

"If you don't believe that the spirit goes on, as I do."

Rosa and I looked at each other non-plussed.

What?

"Fine," Flynn said. "I'm sorry I brought it up."

"You just have no poetry in your soul, Flynn." Smith said, "None."

"Can we just get on with it! Stop being so goddamed unprofessional!"

Smith sighed. "Yes, all right." He aimed the .22 at my left eye, "I'm sure you young people haven't had enough time to really get down to sinning. Once you get to the other side, it'll all be okay."

I did my best to face him unflinchingly, trying to find some way to get out of this, but I saw his trigger finger begin to tighten.

Two shots broke the silence.

CHAPTER TWENTY-SIX

Blood through falling snow.

I wondered why I didn't feel dead, then, as Smith pitched forward, I realized the blood spatter on my face wasn't my own. He lay on his side in the snow, a spreading stain of red growing under him in the fresh powder. All of us, including Flynn, stood and stared a moment, before the remaining assassin, with a panicked expression, started to raise the big pistol towards us.

Two more shots rang out, Flynn joined his partner in the reddening snow.

"Too bad I had to shoot both of 'em," a familiar voice came from the swirling blizzard, "at least Mike here got some good phone footage." A shape materialized out of the swirling flakes.

Jim Three Feathers had saved our lives once again.

He walked up to us, carrying what looked like Teeg Mason's M-4 carbine, and following him were Ronnie and Mike, Pockmark and Handsome from the Daylighter Inn parking lot. They had rifles also. Rosa didn't say a word, she just walked over to Three Feathers, put her arms around him and gave him a hug I felt envious of.

"There, there," he chuckled. "You're safe now, young lady. We was watching for the right moment, and I could see that it arrived when them two started marching you out into the sage brush."

"But…" I said, "How the hell did you know to even be here, much less in the nick of time, Mr. Three Feathers? And don't tell me some magic coyote told you, or I'm gonna probably lose it."

He laughed. "Mac, I hope I can convince you, after all we been through to call me Jim. We were behind you and Rosa here from the time that van turned on to the highway going northeast."

"Nadine told us that Cleeve had you two." He said, "Just damn glad he waited to have these "pros" do it out of his county. We been stayin' back, parking lights only for a hell of a long time. Just followed your van tracks in the snow, 'til you all turned off into this parking area."

"I can't… I… just…" I looked at the Three Feathers, then at the two men who'd come all this way with him. "You guys…"

"Just shut up, man. We get it." Ronnie, formerly Pockmark, said, obviously embarrassed.

Mike, aka Handsome, flashed a bright winning smile. "Eh. You, we didn't care so much about, but we couldn't sit by and let such a pretty girl get it." The smile flashed Rosa's way, and she smiled back. I didn't even care.

I had a debt now, that I doubted I'd ever be able to repay in full.

"What now, Uncle?" Ronnie said, gesturing to the two dead men.

"You wipe down this rifle like I said?"

"Yessir. Took my time, wiped it down good."

Three Feathers, hands wearing leather driving gloves, carefully placed the M-4 next to Flynn, and picked up the .44 magnum he'd been carrying. He stood again and nodded.

"That should confuse everybody. These guys were planning on leaving these young people out here in the snow 'til someone found 'em in the Spring. Now they can have that priviledge. And when they find that rifle, belongin' to the current sheriff, it'll be even more interestin' once they do that ballistics stuff on those wounds."

"Even if all of us'r dead tomorrow," Mike said, "might cause Cleeve some discomfort down the road. His rifle bein' the weapon that killed two guys with fake FBI ID's. Or so we can hope."

"Mister…" Rosa started. Three Feather raised an eyebrow at her, "er.. Jim… we were in Cleeve's squad car with Herman, one of his lackeys, and he said something about getting rid of Lincoln Davies. That deputy is your cousin, isn't he?"

"He is," Three Feathers said, his mouth narrowing to a thin line, "Maybe we all need to go pay ol' Herman a visit."

"You know him?"

"Everyone knows that drug dealing' piece o' shit'" Ronnie said. "I know right where to find that mother--"

"Language!" Three Feathers barked.

Ronnie ducked his head in acknowledgement. "Yes, Uncle. Sorry."

"Don't be sorry, nephew, be better. But you're right. Let's go pay that greasy little man a visit."

"That sounds like a great idea, but," I said, "do any of you have a working cell phone?"

****

While Rosa dialed, I looked through the van and found my pack, our vests, and my knife. My .45 was stashed behind the seat with everything else. As I walked through the still falling snow toward her, I saw Three Feathers pull out the big magnum pistol as he went into one of the pit toilets. When he came out, he didn't have the gun.

"Gil?" I heard Rosa say, "Can you hear me? Reception is lousy where we're at. Good. Listen, we are in a world of hurt up here."

I followed her around as she moved about the snow-covered parking lot, trying to find the point with the best reception, and she had to call back twice when the connection dropped. We had decided to have Rosa make the call, as she had far better credibility with my uncle. I wanted to try to interject while she was talking, but the all-knowing eyebrow shut me down whenever I would make the attempt.

Once she had him convinced and had told the entire story, it took her a while to calm him down, assuring him we were all right.

"No, Gil," she said, "I'm all right. Mac's all right. We're not coming back yet, we need for you to come here. We also need for you to call Halloran, and see if you can get us some real federal law enforcement backup!"

"Tell him about Davies, how we need to keep him alive," I said. This earned me another raised eyebrow, with extreme prejudice.

Rosa continued, "No, Gil. We are needed here. There is some indication that Cleeve is also going to assassinate the one deputy he hasn't corrupted. We're going to stop that. Cleeve has no other deputies, they're... missing... in the mountains. Actually, they're more than missing."

She listened for a few minutes. "Uh huh. Yeah. We can do that. But please get us some backup as soon as humanly possible. Gil, this guy is ruthless and I think he might be borderline insane. We don't know how many people he has working for him. We're not even sure who we can trust, so we really need the FBI up here ASAP. Like I said, there's one deputy back there who we know wasn't compromised, and we believe his life to be in danger."

She listened for a while. "Okay. We'll see you tomorrow, if things go all right. Convince him, Gil. 'Kay. Bye."

"He think he can get Agent Halloran to listen?" I asked.

"Yeah," she said. "I don't know if you know this Mac, but the reason Gil and the FBI guy are so chummy is because Gil actually saved the guy's life once."

"Didn't know that."

"Yep. Get him to tell you the story sometime."

I wanted her to tell me the story right then, but Three Feathers walked up, and pointed towards the old Jeep Cherokee he and his nephews had come in. "You two ready to get outta here?"

"We leaving the van?" Rosa asked.

"Yeah. If someone runs across it out here, I'd bet dollars to donuts that it's stolen. If you look at the government plates on it, they're fake. Painted. Not a bad job either." He said, "And even if someone finds it, I seriously doubt they'll go wandering around in the snow to stumble over our two 'agents' lying out there. Snow's gonna get deep here soon."

We walked over to the Jeep and Mike got behind the wheel. As Ronnie started to get in the passenger seat, the older man cleared his throat, and the embarrassed nephew just said "Sorry Uncle. Wasn't thinking'." Three Feathers rode shotgun.

We hadn't gone far when Rosa turned to me and said, "Got your wallet?"

"Yeah, why?" I said handing it to her.

She looked in it and took out the company credit card.

"Jim? Is there somewhere around here, preferably near, where we can get a decent meal?" she asked.

"Well," he said, a little embarrassed, "There's a tittie bar about ten miles south. They have it outside of any city jurisdiction, and it's a ways from anything, but they have no trouble attracting business."

"How do you know, Uncle?" Mike asked. Both nephews laughed.

"Wasn't born old, you young jackasses. They make a really good burger there. Why?"

"Because," Rosa said, with no humor in her voice I could detect, "if I don't get some food pretty soon, I might just kill and eat all of you."

Three Feathers turned to Mike. "Tittie bar, and step on it!"

CHAPTER TWENTY-SEVEN

"We won't be staying," Rosa told the waitress. "We want all that to go."

After being yet again elbowed by Rosa though, I realized that once more my gaze had drifted to the busty, bored-looking, mostly naked young woman languidly working her way around a brass pole on what stood for a stage in the Longhorn Bar and Grill.

Jim Three Feathers asked Rosa, "So, you think this employer of yours can get the FBI up here? The real FBI?"

"I can almost guarantee it. Probably be here tomorrow, and if we have someplace safe we can all crash, we'll be in on it," She said. "Probably be late tomorrow though. They're based out of Seattle and they'll have to get a warrant for Cleeve's arrest."

Mike came in from the Jeep. "Uncle, I got hold of Nadine. She hasn't been on duty, and Lincoln ain't answering his cell."

"Hope he calls back soon," Three Feathers said. "Cleeve may not know that you two are still alive, but Lincoln has to be questioning him on all these disappearances. The more he questions, the more danger he's in."

"We need to strategize," Mike said. "Ronnie, do you... Ronnie!"

I was glad to see that I was not the only one having trouble keeping his eyes away from the stage.

"Um.. Yeah. What?"

"I said, we need to do some strategizing. What can we do to keep Cleeve from waxing Lincoln and what do we do with these two while we're all waiting?"

"Maybe," Three Feathers said, chuckling, "this isn't the best place for young men to be trying to plan anything. A few too many distractions."

"Amen," Rosa said, giving me a flat look. "We can plan in the car."

"I paid with the credit card. We can leave soon as we get our food," I said.

"Yeah, I noticed the size of the tip you left. Really, Mac?" Rosa said.

"Uncle Gil can afford to be generous."

****

Driving back toward Loman County, I once again focused on the waxed paper wrapper in front of me, and was mildly heartbroken to see that my burger and ninety percent of my french fries were gone. I covertly looked at Rosa's fries, but was stopped cold by a look that said 'Just try it,' and began cleaning up my own pitiful remnants.

"Maybe we could all stay with my cousin, Katrina," Ronnie said.

"Katrina's got two little boys that are keeping her run ragged while Joseph's in Afghanistan," Three Feathers said. "Let's not add to her burden. I was thinking maybe we should take these two to stay with Auntie Letta."

Both Ronnie and Mike looked at the older man as if he'd gone mad.

"Auntie Letta!?" Ronnie said. Both he and Mike looked at Rosa and me, as if looking for something they hadn't seen before. "You know that she'll--"

"Yeah," Three Feathers interrupted, "I know. Let it be."

"Something we should know, Jim?" I asked.

"Nope. Gonna take you two to stay the night with my great-aunt." Three Feathers looked at me very pointedly. "Maybe you can help her with her chores."

"Um... sure. Always glad to help out," I said.

"Me too," Rosa said.

"Rosa," the older man said, "you and me'll just sit in the house. Maybe drink some coffee, and Auntie makes a mean coffee cake. Mac can help her."

It didn't sound like a suggestion.

We drove on, and I still wasn't sure which county we were in, though if I guessed, I would have said Okanogan. The snow had finally calmed down for a while, and afternoon sunshine made the new snow sparkle. I could see the small birds that wintered in the area starting to show themselves as we drove down the road, and tracks from small animals criss-crossed the fields.

The counties on the east side of the Cascade Mountain range usually have pretty good snow plowing on the roadways, and our way was clear until we finally hit a side road that hadn't seen a plow.

"I don't think I can get to Auntie Letta's without chainin' up, Uncle," Mike said. "I got four-wheel and I can get us up the road to her turn off, but I still ain't put my snow tires on."

"That don't surprise me," Three Feathers said, and Mike looked down at his steering wheel for a moment. "Just get us as close as you can. Me and these two, we're used to walkin' through snow."

We drove up the road a couple of miles, passing orchards full of dormant apple trees, support poles stacked around them like tipis. The Cherokee drove on, sometimes fishtailing, until we came to an intersection with a narrow road that wound around a hill. Mike pulled the Jeep over and painstakingly turned around. Three Feathers opened his door when the vehicle was facing the other way and signaled for Rosa and me to exit.

"All right, nephews," he said, "you know what to do. Don't let Herman see you comin', and get help from the cousins if'n you have to. I don't want him too badly damaged, we need to get information from him, if we're gonna find out what Cleeve's plans are. 'Sides, it's gonna be harder for Lincoln to look the other way if we kidnap this jackass and he's all beat to hell or brain damaged."

'We ain't stupid as you think we are, Uncle," Ronnie said. It struck me that some of the issues between my Uncle Gil and myself were more universal than I thought.

"Just be careful, and don't get killed or caught. Your mamas would skin me if I got you into more trouble."

Wow. Does that sound familiar.

"Mac, Rosa, we got a little hike up to Auntie's house. Let's get a move on while the sun's still shinin'."

The trek up the narrow side road was brisk, to say the least, and I was glad we were walking in sunshine. After sitting for a few hours, all the soreness caused by our adventures had come to the fore, and looking over, I could see Rosa was moving stiffly too. Sleeping in a bed tonight would be just short of heaven.

We passed several older houses and a couple of newer ones including a 'McMansion' complete with faux tower. As we got farther out, the houses became few and far between and at the end of the road, we finally came to an old cabin. It was sturdily built, with a stone and concrete foundation and a green metal roof that I would have bet good money was built over an older shake roof. Metal plant hangers held pots filled with a few die-hard flowers that hadn't quite realized winter was here and a concrete paver pathway to the place had been recently shoveled.

Three Feathers walked up hand hewn log steps to a generous porch and started to knock on a door made of thick old planks. Before his knuckle could contact the wood, the door swung in and a face with the ages imprinted on it looked out at us.

"Auntie," Jim said, "I brought—"

"Yeah," she said, "I know. You come in now, outta dat cold. Kick them boots off at the door. Don' wanna have to sweep one more time again."

We walked across thin worn carpet to a linoleum-floored kitchen straight out of the 1950s, everything clean and gleaming. There was an old style metal coffee pot, one of the kind with the percolator on top, and it was plugged in and starting to perk. Evidently, she wasn't kidding about expecting us.

Jim pulled three coffee cups from the cupboard as if he was quite familiar with their placement and poured coffee for himself and Rosa. When I started to reach for the pot, he put his hand out.

"Later, son. Right now, Auntie needs for you to help her outside."

"I... Uh... Okay, no problem."

Auntie pointed toward the back door leading out of the kitchen, and retrieving my boots, I followed her out. The backyard was just as eclectic as the front, with hanging wind chimes and planters full of flowers starting to wilt in the cold. A forest trail led up into the mountains behind the cabin and huge old pines towered over everything. A small creek meandered thirty feet to the side of the place.

The old woman, who, if she was Jim Three Feathers' great aunt had to at least be in her nineties, moved like a much younger person. There was none of the glassy fragility that people developed in their eighties, and the bright eyes in that weathered face looked as sharp as someone much younger. Actually sharper than many younger people I knew.

"We dig these potatoes, here." She pointed at some odd tall terra cotta pots with holes all along the sides and handed me a pair of work gloves. "Just dig 'em out with yer hands, put 'em in this bag."

I nodded, and began digging in the first pot. Soon I was pulling sizable potatoes out and once I had the thing down, my mind was able to relax. I worked and watched my surroundings, something that had been pounded into my head by wilderness teachers and trackers. Don't focus everything in one place.

"What you hear, boy?"

"Just listening to that chickadee, over in the choke cherry. He's tellin' everyone all about it."

"What he sayin'?"

I looked at her, the expression she gave me was very serious, intense.

"Ah.. Well, I think he's saying 'Hey, winter, I'm still here. 'I'm not leavin' and I'm not worried. Bring it on' is what it sounds like."

I saw just a flicker of a smile, then the old woman's expression fell back to neutral. We started to dig more potatoes. I breathed in and she looked over at me.

"Whatchoo smell?"

"Smell?"

"Yeah. You were breathin' in and I guess your nose ain't fell off. What you smell?"

"Air smells... wet, and cold. I think we'll have more snow coming in at nightfall."

"What else? Breathe deep. Smell deep."

"The pines... wait... the cows smell..." I looked up the hillside, directly into the eyes of a female elk. "Well! Hello there! Guess I must be down wind of you." The elk looked at me dismissively at such an inane comment and walked up the hill.

"Guess your nose ain't dead after all," Auntie said.

"No ma'am." I was pretty sure after that moment that I'd always be able to tell when an elk was near.

"Keep digging, boy. You like bein' outside?"

"More than just about anything. I always feel like I'm... I dunno... home."

She gestured out towards the valley. "Things have moved on for most people. They got their TVs and their jobs and their things, but what they don't got is now-time in their heads. You outside for a while, you can get into now-time. You know what I say?"

"Uh...not exactly..."

"People always in then-time. I'll be alive *then*, after I do this thing and that thing. Later, they wonder where all the time they had went. It went to then, stuff that might happen or stuff that's already happened. Life goes on by, but their mind's only half there. Not paying attention. Out here, you just need a few good things to keep warm, safe, and fed, not a ton o' stuff to steal your now from you."

"You can't live outside all the time though," I said.

"When I was a little girl, we didn't have a log house. Just had tents. I like this house. I been livin' there a long time, but I spend most of my days out here, even when it's cold. The world talks to me out here. It don't so much in there." She gestured at my sack of potatoes. "That's enough taters. We go in now. She's seen what she needs to."

"Who?"

"Never mind. Let's go have us some coffee and cake."

CHAPTER TWENTY-EIGHT

It was well after dark when Herman came to visit.

I guess, technically, you can call someone a visitor if they're carried in the front door over someone's shoulder, hands, feet and mouth duct taped together. Our visitor didn't look too happy to be there, the bruises on his face being sort of a giveaway.

"Any trouble findin' him?" Three Feathers asked.

"Naw, Uncle," Mike said, coming in the door. "Herman's a creature of habit. We found him at the White Owl gettin' plastered. He was more'n willin' to sell us something illegal in the parking lot."

Ronnie dropped him off his shoulder, letting Herman land on his feet and guided the hopping captive to a sturdy-looking oak chair. Herman was barely seated before Mike had a rope through the back of the chair and looped around the man's rather dirty neck. Jim Three Feathers pulled up another chair, sat down in front of him and sighed.

"Herman, you have been a very bad man. You work for an even worse one." He said, "Ron, would you get that tape off his mouth so he can talk."

"Sure, Uncle." Ronnie pulled the tape off. He did it quickly and he wasn't particularly gentle about it.

"Ahhhh! Damn!" Herman cried out, "Have a heart would you?"

Much to everyone's surprise, Rosa came flying off the couch, her anger like standing too close to a superheated wood stove. "Have a heart? You set us up, gave us over to men who were going to leave us dead behind the outhouses. You *bolsa de mierda!*" Before anyone could stop her, she had fired a slap to Herman's face, not the stinging kind of slap, but one that glazed his eyes over for a moment.

I stepped between them, and even I was a little taken aback at the blazing fury in her eyes, and I was pissed at the son of a bitch too.

"Okay, Rosa," I said quietly. "You've got his attention, now let Jim talk to him. All right?"

"He set us up, Mac. They would have killed you like a dog!"

"I'm alive and well, sweetheart. Let's sit down and listen a while." Rosa sat, but if looks could kill, Herman would have needed a funeral plot.

Order restored, Three Feathers continued. "The young lady's got a point Herman, you haven't exactly made friends in this room. I would keep the whinin' to a minimum if'n I was you. You ain't gonna get much sympathy here."

"What is it you people want?"

"You said some things in front of these two young folks here, just before sending them to their assumed deaths. Said there was plans for my cousin Lincoln. I'd like to know those plans, please."

Whatever drunkenness Herman had been cultivating had evaporated under the drive here and the ringing slap to his face. You could almost see the duplicity in his eyes as he tried to come up with a suitable lie. His first effort showed his level of creativity.

"Hell, I don't even know what you all are talkin' about."

"Please, Jim," Rosa said from the couch, "give me five minutes with him, that's all I'm asking."

"You can have your shot, if he keeps lyin' to me, Rosa." Three Feathers said, looking pointedly at Herman. "Let me see if I can spare ol' Herm here a little agony first."

He didn't get the chance. We were all surprised when Auntie walked up to Herman, looked him in the eye and said, "You tell Jim here what we need to know about what that Cleeve is thinkin' for my other grand-nephew. You tell him, or you fertilize the corn for next year."

"I ain't gonna help you with yer dang garden, Gramma! I'm a white man, I ain't yer slave."

"Herman," I said, explaining slowly and carefully, "I think she means you'll *be* the fertilizer, if you get my meaning."

Our captive's face went white. "You wouldn't do that, now. It ain't right."

"I been alive a long time. Long time," Auntie said, "I seen many bad things done, terrible things. I don't feel too bad if bad things come to white men who do bad things. You tell him! You tell him now, or I go get cleaver and fix you!"

"Please, Herman," Jim said, "let me help you here. She's not kidding. She knows the three S's."

"Three S's?" Herman asked, his voice quavering a little.

"You know, 'Shoot, Shovel, Shut Up. Those."

"I… you wouldn't! You wouldn't dare!"

"What I got to lose?" she screeched, "I'm old! My nephew, he young."

"I ain't…" Herman started.

"That's it! I had enough!" Auntie yelled in a voice much louder and sharper than I would have thought someone her age could generate. "Grandson," she said to Ronnie, "go get that blue tarp out of da shed."

"Yes, Auntie!" Ronnie left the room.

"I go sharpen cleaver now," She told Jim. As she walked by us, facing away from Herman, she gave Rosa and me a big burlesque wink.

"Shit, Herman," Jim said, looking towards the retreating Auntie with a deeply concerned expression on his face. "Now you gone and done it."

"Wha.. Hunh… You…" Herman had just about lost coherency, even though the effect of whatever he'd been drinking was long gone.

"Please, son, just give me something. I need to hear the truth. I don't want my great auntie to go to prison, so we'll wind up havin' to bury *you* real deep in the dirt. She grew up in the old days, man. She's only part civilized." Three Feathers looked again toward the kitchen, winking at Rosa as he did it. "Don't make this happen!"

Herman looked at me. "You can't let these injuns do this! Not to another white man! Help me!"

I picked up a toothpick I'd been using to remove coffee cake from my teeth, dangled it on my lip and gave Herman my best Phillip Marlowe impression.

"I didn't mean nothin' to you earlier, buttercup. What makes you think you mean anything to me?"

His stricken expression told me that Herman didn't have much resistance left, but the final straw came from the kitchen. The sound of steel being dragged over a sharpening stone came clearly and Herman's will collapsed, along with his bladder control.

"I'll tell you what I know! Cleve didn't tell me everything. He don't tell no one everything, but I swear, everything I know! Just keep that ol' woman away from me!"

"Well, I wish you'd of done that before pissing on her chair," Three Feathers said, exasperation in his voice, "That ain't gonna help no one here. Now, you said there was a plan for my cousin Lincoln. I want to know what it is, and I want to know right now."

"Cleeve and Lincoln Davies are the only two officers left in the department, 'cept for a couple part-timers. Lincoln's pretty suspicious of Cleeve's story and keeps talkin' about bringing in outsiders for an investigation."

"I see. And Cleeve's little fantasy won't stand up well to outside scrutiny, will it?"

"Uh, maybe... not..." Herman glanced nervously toward the kitchen.

"What's he going to do?" Rosa asked, her expression bleak.

"Keepin' it simple. Deputy goes out on a call, they find his body and squad car, the scene of some scuffle with a bad guy. Deputy bein' the loser."

"Ah!" a voice came from the kitchen. "Nice an' sharp!"

"Oh dear God! Make her stop that! Make her stop!"

"Auntie," Jim said, turning in his chair, "I think Herman's going to cooperate now, no need for the cleaver."

"Oh." The disappointment in that one word should have given Auntie the Academy Award for best actress that year.

At least... I think she was acting...

"Any other plans you know of, Herman?" I asked, "Now is not the time to hold anything back."

"All I know is the general plan, man. We make a shitload of meth, Cleeve coverin' our asses. Then sell it across the mountains, bank it offshore and split for foreign countries down the road with new identities."

"Hell," Jim said, "I bet you got your Canadian ID papers already!"

Herman wouldn't look him in the eye.

"I hate you bastards," Rosa said, her voice choking. "Destroying people's lives for profit!"

"Herman," Three Feathers said, "I want you to answer me honestly, not for me, but for you. Knowing everything you know now, and I will tell you that the FBI is gonna probably be here tomorrow or the next day, what do you think is goin' to happen to Cleeve's little house of cards?"

Herman looked like a little kid about to be grounded. Staring at the floor, he said, "I guess everything's gonna fall to shit, ain't it?"

"I don't see any other way for it to shake out. But what's going to happen to you? What's gonna be Herman's fate? He gonna go down with his truly nasty boss, or is he gonna be a good guy?"

"What? Good guy? How?"

'When the feds get here, ol' Herman is ready and willing to not only sign a confession for being in on Cleeve's business, but he tells them every detail of his operations. We all here, just conveniently forget about you being complicit in the attempted murder of these two young people and—"

"What the HELL, Jim!?" This time I was the one off the couch.

"Now listen, Mac, we need to get Cleeve behind bars. Herman's just a flunky," he turned toward the tied man, "no offense, Herman. He can write out everything he knows, and when them federal boys get here, he's standin' waiting to meet them, to tell them more than they even want to know."

"What's in it for me?" Herman asked.

"You don't get charged as accomplice to murder, dumbass," I said. "Likely, you get a little time for dealin' but the feds might even give you immunity for your testimony. They're gonna want Cleeve bad, and Rosa, Jim, and I might not be enough vindication for them. They'll want every nail in the coffin they can get."

"Okay," Herman said, misery in his voice, "but God help me if Cleeve finds out."

CHAPTER TWENTY-NINE

"Get up, son! Get your shoes on! We gotta move now!"

"Whuh.. Hunh?" I sat up on the lumpy couch. I had been dreaming of a dark woman-shaped figure standing over me, eyes glowing. Just standing there, watching...

Herman jerked awake in his chair, looking as bleary as I felt. Fortunately for him, Three Feathers had let him clean up and he was wearing a battered pair of jeans belonging to a nephew I hadn't met. Of course, the tape had gone back on his hands once all needs were met.

Three Feathers stood at the end of the couch, and beyond him I could see Rosa and Ronnie, both sleepy-eyed, gratefully taking cups of coffee from Auntie Letta. I went into the kitchen, splashed cold water onto my face and was almost sent to Nirvana when she handed me mine.

"Okay, I'm awake, sorta. What's happening?"

"Had a call from Nadine. Dispatch just sent Lincoln to check out a fight going on at Little Manitou campground," Jim told us.

"Little Manitou? Why would anyone be up there? It's snowing again!" Mike asked, coming out of the bathroom. Three Feathers looked at him with an 'are you kidding me' look.

"Cleeve."

"Yes, nephew, I'd say it's a good bet. You and Ronnie are gonna drive us... did you get your snow tires on?"

"Before we went to retrieve Leaky here," Mike said, gesturing towards Herman.

"Good. Me an' these two," he said, gesturing at Rosa and me, "are gonna stay back in the back seats. Maybe it is something innocent, and Lincoln will just be there to do his job. But from what we know, it sounds mighty suspicious. And hey," he said, looking at Ronnie, "why didn't he call us?"

"From what Nadine said, Cleeve's been running his ass ragged," Ronnie said. "Been on shift for over twenty-four hours. He don't call back lot o' the time, anyway. Probably just blowin' me off."

"Hope that don't get him blown away," Three Feathers said in a grim tone.

***

This wasn't how I wanted this to happen.

If we were going to interfere with that crafty bull of a bastard, Dominic Cleeve, I wanted to have the FBI, the State Patrol, hell… even the National Guard at my back. Instead, I had a sixty-something Native American man and his two nephews, one of which I had dropped with a single side kick. I had Rosa, whose skill I respected more than anyone else present, including myself, but I hated the thought of the danger to her.

Of course, thinking that I was taking her into this was probably a foolish bit of hubris. If I'd had both legs broken, she would have still gone with Jim and the nephews even if I was left behind

Rosa, Jim and myself were crammed into the back seat of the Cherokee, baseball caps pulled low over our brows when we pulled out on the road from Auntie's. For a moment, I worried a little that we might get pulled over by a state patrol, and not be able to explain the situation well enough to get help for Lincoln Davies. I needn't have worried. The WSP's resources were always stretched, and after the last snows, most of their officers were trying to keep order on the highways in more populated areas of the state.

"Gil?" Rosa said into her freshly charged phone, "We gotta bit of a problem. How soon are you and the feds goin' to get here? What? Oh shit." She listened for a moment. "Look Gil, we think the sole remaining deputy who was not on this Cleeve guy's corruption train is about to be assassinated. No, I'm serious."

I could hear my uncle's vocal volume rise, though I couldn't make out the words. I saw Rosa's body language change, and I was certain Uncle Gil had crossed the line in his demands.

"No, Gil, we are not coming home now. I don't care." Rosa

continued. "No, you listen to me. This man Cleeve has used murder to remove everyone in his path, and he's about to do it again to the last honest lawman up here. No. We're going. Tell your fed friends that this is coming to a head and they need to expedite, as in getting their asses moving. No. Goodbye, Gil."

Rosa cut the connection, and sat for a moment.

"He's pissed, I take it?" I said.

"Oh yeah. Wants us to get into the company car and get our butts outta this county. Maybe if the stakes weren't so high with Davies, I might think he was right," she said.

I thought so too. We were about to engage in a form of vigilante action that if it didn't land us in jail, might at least make us lose our legal standing in the fugitive retrieval business. But the truth was, both Rosa and myself had a lot more training in just about everything in this business than Jim and his nephews, and if we walked away, there was more than a fair chance that Cleeve might win and Lincoln Davies might die.

"There's one other thing, Rosa," I said. "I'm not for a moment going to say it's the smartest thought I've ever had, but this son of a bitch tried very hard to kill us on multiple occasions. I'm not about to let him kill one more innocent person. If we can get there in time, maybe Lincoln can vouch for us. If not, at least we can make sure Cleeve goes down for it."

"Hell, yeah," she said.

"We'll get there in time," Three Feathers said. I wasn't sure if he was reassuring us, or himself.

****

The snow started coming down again.

We did make one stop on the way. At a public mailbox on the edge of town, Ronnie got out of the Jeep and deposited three different letters: one from myself and Rosa, one from Herman, and one from Jim Three Feathers. All were addressed to FBI agent Jake Halloran, Uncle Gil's friend and contact with the bureau. In the event things went completely south, the affidavits were at least going to be getting to someone in authority.

"These are our 'dead man switch' method of making sure Cleeve gets his," I said.

"We ain't gonna need 'em, but always good to have a backup," Rosa replied.

The trip to Little Manitou campground was made in general silence, each person lost in their own thoughts, perhaps of what the future would bring, today and beyond. I sat next to Rosa, trying to only concentrate on counting each breath. That probably seems like an odd thing to do, but I wanted to be completely cool when we got there, not keyed up to the point of making stupid mistakes.

Three Feathers' face was like a stone mask, betraying nothing, and beside me, Rosa was watching the snow fall like a hawk watches a distant dove. Ronnie and Mike, from what I could see from the back seat, just looked worried.

"Here's the turnoff," Ronnie told Mike, who just looked at him with an irritated expression.

"Yeah, man. Been here before, ain't I?"

"Mike," Three Feathers said, "pull over there."

We stopped and all got out of the Cherokee, looking at the entrance to Little Manitou Campground Road. We were past camping season, and the road showed only one set of tracks in the snow. They were either pickup or SUV tracks.

"Doesn't Lincoln drive a squad car?" Rosa asked.

"Not in weather like this. In winter, especially to a place out of the way, the sheriffs use one of the two new SUVs they got last year." Mike explained.

"There's only been one vehicle been driven through here," Three Feathers said, hope starting to trickle into his voice. "Maybe we ain't too late. In the truck, everyone!"

We headed up the road, though I wasn't particularly comfortable with it. If Cleeve was going to show, we were leaving another set of tracks.

The drive in to the campground only took about ten minutes, even with the almost axle-deep snow. Sitting there waiting was a shiny SUV with the Loman County Sheriff Department logo on the front doors. It had parked at the first campsite, the farthest place to be plowed, and a set of bootprints continued on the snowy loop road that fed to all the other campsites in the area.

"Let's get out here," Jim said, "everything looks okay, but it might be better to not rush in announcing our presence."

We emerged from the Jeep, everyone retrieving their part of our mis-matched arsenal of weapons and began to follow Lincoln Davies trail.

"Why'd he leave his truck?" Ronnie asked, "Obviously ain't no one been out here."

"Could be snow campers, snowmobilers, cross country skiers, out here, maybe parked elsewhere?" Rosa said.

"Snow's been coming down pretty good," Ronnie said, "so anyone could be out here, and their tracks wouldn't necessarily show."

"No one's been here since it began snowing," I said. Jim Three Feathers nodded.

"Lincoln a tracker?" Rosa asked him.

"Naw. A good man, but don't follow the old ways to any extent."

"Let's not speculate, and just go find him," I said.

We started our investigation of the campground, following the fresh tracks. Three Feathers and the nephews each carried deer rifles while Rosa carried my .45. I'd been given an old Colt .44, a cowboy style pistol in a worn leather belt holster. I felt a little like Billy the Kid, but I really hoped I wouldn't wind up going against anyone out here with a long gun.

We walked in silence, and after a night's semi-rest and a good meal, I was able to appreciate how beautiful the falling snow was again. With no one talking, the only sound was that of our boots moving through the new snow, with one exception. Even with what amounted to a winter storm, I could hear the little birds, Juncos and Chickadees, singing and chirping in the cold. I could concentrate on their quiet little homage to the Creator of All Things and it kept my mind from spinning into overdrive.

Being in overdrive was how you missed things.

This campground evidently was a major one. We passed through an RV section, then a natural area, then another RV section, all with electric and water hookups. Moving through a part that was labeled for tenting, we finally came to a big open area which I guessed was for kids to play in, judging from the playground equipment in the center. There was also a sign pointing at the far end to a trail leading into the forest, which announced that it was the Manitou Lake Loop Trail. Davies' prints were headed in that direction.

"Where the hell is he going?" Mike asked.

"Up that trail, obviously," Ronnie replied.

"But why?"

"Where does this loop come out?" I asked.

Three Feathers looked at me, alarm in his expression. "Goes up to the lake. There's also a loop comes out at Devil Creek campground, about five miles up the road."

"What would make a law officer go tramping up a lonely trail?" I said.

"How about gunshots in the distance?" Rosa said. "He's a lawman. If someone was shooting out there, he'd likely go to investigate."

Three Feathers eyes grew wide. "Let's get goin'! Double time."

We set off at a fast trot, dragging ourselve through calf-deep snow, and I was glad that Rosa had started me on trail running. We'd barely gone a thousand yards and I started to hear both Ronnie and Mike breathing hard. Another ten minutes and they were both falling behind. Three Feathers took a second to glare at them.

"You two catch up when you can. Ronnie! Give this boy your rifle."

"Best give it to Rosa, she's a better shot," I said.

Rosa took the rifle and ten cartridges. I noticed she didn't offer the .45 to Ronnie. For a moment, I thought about asking Mike for his rifle too, but didn't want to leave the two of them out here unarmed.

Rosa, Jim and I started up the trail again.

Five minutes later, we heard shots ahead of us.

CHAPTER THIRTY

There's a terrible price to be paid when you've been shot at a few times. You never quite see the world in the same way again. There is always a consciousness that something moving at very high speed might impact your body in a very detrimental way. When you actually hear shots, your defense mechanisms go into high gear.

I won't say the world slowed down, but everything, as we ran towards the sound of gunfire, seemed to grow crystal clear, each snowflake taking on a special luster. Perhaps that luster was fueled by the knowledge of our own temporary nature.

The forest had opened into a meadow, the trail running almost through the center, and through the snow, lying next to a log, I could see a shape on the ground. It was a man shape.

"Goddam it," Three Feathers said in a hushed tone. "Too late!"

I was scanning the area, trying to find an active shooter, when I heard Rosa say, "He's still alive!"

I looked, and saw the man shape raise up from behind the log, seeming to point toward the trees to the north. His pointing became a firearm, shooting in that direction. Lincoln Davies was still in the game.

"Yes!" I said, "Lincoln's shooting back!"

A muzzle flash appeared in the dim light from the trees where Lincoln had aimed. Davies dropped back down behind the log. I couldn't see the shooter through the heavy snow fall.

"Okay, you two," Jim said, keeping as quiet as he could, "let's see if we can come around on Cleeve's flank here and jump him. Quiet as we can."

We moved into the forest near our position, then began an eternity of moving through snow-covered brush and logs, trying to get into a better position without warning our prey. I move pretty well in the woods, and I was having some trouble keeping quiet but even with her athleticism, Rosa was having a hard time avoiding snapping limbs. Fortunately, the falling snow seemed to muffle even the sound of gunshots.

Jim Three Feathers didn't make a sound. I still had much to learn.

We'd expected to sneak up on Cleeve, and I assumed, get the drop on him, hopefully forcing him to surrender to superior numbers. That was the plan in my mind.

Cleeve evidently hadn't received the memo. The only warning that I got that we were now engaged was Three Feathers frantically signaling for Rosa and I to take cover while he did his best to conceal himself behind a tree far too small.

A shape came running toward us, like an arctic Batman.

Cleeve, wearing a white and dark green surplus snow camouflage poncho, appeared out of the falling snow, seeming to not see us immediately. I began to yell out for him to drop his weapon, as I aimed my pistol at him. Jim Three Feathers had a different idea. He rose up, took aim, and fired his 30-.06 rifle, hitting the white shape dead center. Cleeve went over backward in the snow and lay still.

"Jesus, Jim!" Rosa said, "He had no chance to surrender."

"Wasn't gonna take the chance," he said with a grim tone. "Son of a bitch is too slippery by half. Far as I'm concerned, he didn't give us a choice."

Jim wasn't giving us much of a choice either. Either we lied, or we condemned this man who had saved our lives to a possible prison term. I looked at Dominic Cleeve, lying on the ground as we started to move forward.

Nope. Cleeve, you're not worth Jim Three Feathers.

Looking at him, I noted one other thing. There was no blood. There should have been a lot.

"He's faking!" I yelled. "Get back!" As I called out, Cleeve sat up, and began unloading at us with a handgun, semi-auto, and we all dove for cover.

I heard Rosa cry out, and my blood went cold. I began firing at Cleeve with the old revolver as fast as it would shoot, but our assailant was up and moving, running in the opposite direction, firing back at us as he could. I fired again, and heard a metallic sound. Cleeve stumbled, but kept running.

"Rosa!" I scrambled through the snow to where she was holding the front of right her leg. Blood was seeping between her fingers, but it wasn't pouring out in a gush.

"Son of a bitch must've had a vest on! He pulled a page from your book, kids," Three Feathers said.

"I'm all right, dammit!" Rosa slapped my hand as I tried to see. "He hit me in the front of my quad just as I was turning back for cover. Give me your bandage."

I reached behind me and fished my trauma bandage from my butt pack and stripped it out of its wrapping. Rosa grabbed it from my hand. "Jim, you and Mac get that son of a bitch! Mac, take this rifle and leave me your pistol."

"I can't leave you here, bleeding in the snow!"

"I'll be okay. It's just a hole through the front of my quadriceps muscle. Hurts like hell, but not bleeding too bad. Mike and Ronnie weren't that far behind us, and Lincoln is down in the meadow. The shot will bring them here, and I'll be fine."

"Rosa…"

"Mac! Don't you let him get away! Not after all he's done!" She said, "Jim! Get him moving!"

"C'mon, son. We got a bad man to take care of," Jim said softly.

I handed Rosa the pistol and belt with its extra rounds. She handed me the rifle and the extra cartridges then said, "Be careful, Mac. Don't let him kill you or I'll be really upset with you."

"Can't have that. See you soon, baby." I kissed her, rose, and nodded to Three Feathers. We set out at a trot, following Cleeve's obvious trail in the snow.

****

We doggedly followed our prey, and to tell the truth, it felt good to think of Dominic Cleeve as prey. I wasn't for a moment forgetting what a dangerous man we were after, but with the skills of both Three Feathers and myself, I thought we had a good chance of taking him down. Nothing I'd seen of Cleeve led me to believe he was more than a mediocre outdoorsman and everything I'd seen of Jim Three Feathers told me he was a great backwoodsman.

We moved along fairly quickly, barely needing to glance down at the trough through the snow that was Cleeve's back trail. As we had moved away from the shooting area, the juncos and chickadees once again started singing their brave winter songs.

"He's heading towards the loop trail, I think. Probably got a car at the other lot," I said.

"Yeah." Three Feathers agreed, "Even if we lose him here, he's finished. Even with the snow, Lincoln must've seen who was shootin' at him. This, and all the other stuff mounting against him, you know he's been sloppy and it's only a matter of time before he's behind bars."

"You think he knows that?"

"Who knows? Cleeves been acting like he's invincible, and that don't seem too sane to me," Jim said, "If Lincoln was dead, Cleeve would've been the only sheriff left, besides a couple part-timers, and would have strong-armed things, maybe givin' himself time to fake evidence. That's all gonna ring false if one of his own people starts callin' him out and questioning everything."

"So what's his play?"

"Far as I can see, the only thing he's got left is escape. There's several dirt roads that go over the border into Canada. My guess is he'll abandon whatever vehicle he's got, slip over, and in a few months, resurface with a new identity, maybe one with a big ol' beard."

"We need to get to him before he gets back to his car."

"If we don't want him to get away. I'd guess he's got some sort of rig there at the other campground, maybe somethin' unofficial with big tires and 4-wheel drive. Maybe somethin' that has all his bug-out stuff ready to go at a moment's notice."

We moved on, soon hitting the loop trail, and the length of Cleeve's strides extended out far between each step as he increased his pace. Fifteen minutes later, having not caught up with him, we came to a fork in the trail. The tracks turned to the right, and Jim Three Feathers began to laugh, and laugh hard.

"Jim, what the hell's so funny? We've been after him long enough that he must be getting close to the other campground!"

"Nope," he replied. "You're a tracker, carefully look at that trail that goes to the left."

I did, and I realized that Cleeve must've been waiting for Lincoln for some time. There was, upon close examination, the faint remains of a track-trail coming up from the direction I was examining. The falling snow had all but erased it, but it was there if you looked closely. I looked at Three Feathers, wanting to ask the question, but he answered before I opened my mouth.

"He was in a hurry, and his memory played a trick on him. He took the right fork going in, and coming out, he took the right fork too."

"When he should have taken the left, coming back. Where's that trail go?" I asked, gesturing toward where Cleeve's tracks continued.

"Oh, up to Little Manitou Lake. It's about ten miles up in the mountains." He paused for effect. "This is also the only trail back out."

I felt the grin begin, and it was impossible to rein it in. For a few moments, Three Feathers and I just laughed.

Laughed like fools.

****

The trail to the lake was gradual, but it definitely gained elevation. We were climbing sets of long slippery switchbacks, trying to keep an eye uphill, in case we saw Cleeve coming down. His trail doggedly kept going, but I was seeing stuttering hesitations that led me to believe he was starting to realize his mistake.

We came to a turn, where the trail doubled back, one angle coming up from below, the other going onward up the hill, and I saw that Cleeve had stopped, looking back down the valley where we had all come from.

He knew we were following. His vantage point looked right down at the trail we'd been coming up.

"Shit." was all Jim Three Feathers said. No further discussion was needed.

We were on high alert as we continued. We passed a huge tangle of old logs and had our rifles ready in case Cleeve was using them as an ambush point.

Nothing.

His trail continued on and up. We were both good in the woods, there was no way Cleeve was going to ambush us, so he was probably trying to make a run for it. All in vain. Maybe he'd share the same fate as his deputies, even if we didn't find him.

The wilderness in winter isn't forgiving of mistakes, as we soon learned.

The first inkling we had that he was near was when a medium sized log came flying down the hill. I glimpsed Cleeve in his camo poncho, lying above us where he'd kicked the wooden missile down the hill and even had a split second to wonder why he hadn't used the handgun.

"Jim! Look out!" Whether the old wolves would ever want to admit it or not, there is an advantage in youth. I twisted and did a wild sort of dive over the top of the log as it came at us, but Three Feathers was not fast enough to get out of the way. He tried to jump over it as it came at him and hooked a foot on it as it passed underneath him. The next thing I knew, he was rolling down the hill, rifle flying, following Cleeve's wooden booby trap.

I barely noted this, as I was rammed by Cleeve's huge bulk. He had come to his feet and sprinted down the hill and taken me hard as any NFL linebacker. Had I not managed to get my rifle between us, I probably would have broken several ribs. Hitting the weapon was painful for us both, and I heard wood crack at the impact. I slid down the trail on my back. The only thing that saved me from getting the stomping of the century was the impact made him lose his footing in the snow as well.

He came at me again, pistol in one hand. There was no way I could get the rifle up in time.

I'm dead.

Instead of shooting me, however, he swung the weapon at my head, and I blocked with the rifle. On impact, part of the handgun flew off into the snow. Evidently I had hit his pistol, and not him when he'd fled earlier and it was too damaged to shoot. I snapped the rifle butt at him, hoping to use it like a club and he knocked it out of my hand like a gorilla swatting a monkey. It went flying. I arrowed a good hard straight punch at his throat, and made good contact. His bull neck muscles protected him, but he went to one knee, coughing, giving me a second to get set for the next onslaught.

"It's too late, Cleeve! You've done too much, man. Piled it too high and deep. You're gonna get what you deserve!"

"What I deserve, you skinny little fuck, is to have a fancy home and a huge-boobed blonde in Belize," he almost screamed. "And you're in my fucking way!"

He flung back one side of the poncho, and came off the ground like a charging bull. I started to set up to give him a good hard stopping side kick.

Don't be so predictable, Mac.

Sempai Dade's words again went through my head, and I dropped as the big man came in. Spinning in a 180 degree arc as I landed, I caught him on the side of his knee with a very low spinning heel kick. The reaping blow took both feet out from under him, and he went sideways, out over the incline Three Feathers had tumbled down earlier, the poncho tangling him up as he went.

He couldn't get any purchase on the hillside and slid as far as the next section of trail below us. He was tough. It couldn't have been very easy on the body sliding and tumbling that far, but he got to his feet, and looked down the trail. There was no one between him and his car now, and looking up the hill, he grinned at me and started trotting toward the other campground.

He only has to get across the border and disappear.

I started frantically looking for my rifle, lost in the deepening snow, but it had gone far and probably wouldn't be seen 'til spring.

"Mac!" I heard Three Feathers below. He was limping on to the trail from a snow-covered clump of brush. "Get down here and give me a hand! My foot is bunged up pretty bad."

I slid down the hill, my boots almost acting as skis and stopped on the trail below. Moving to Three Feathers, I put my arm around him, and we began hobbling down the trail. There was no way I was going to catch Cleeve like this, but I couldn't leave Jim up here in a snowstorm.

"I feel like I should run after him." I said, "He's gonna make it out of here."

"Can't be helped. Be a bad idea to try and take him alone, and my rifle needs a good cleaning before I'd feel safe firing it again."

The frustration boiled up. "Shit!" I yelled to the snow-filled world. Jim was right, we'd saved Lincoln, and there was a very good chance Cleeve would stomp a mud-hole in my butt if I went after him solo.

But letting the man escape left a bitter taste in my mouth.

In retrospect, I probably should have noted the juncos and chickadees had stopped calling. A growl that came from just down hill of the section of trail we were on, was easily recognizable for anyone who's spent a great deal of time in the mountains.

Growl of a bear. And a very irritated growl at that.

The North Cascades, which the Pasayten Wilderness adjoins, has a funny little secret. It has grizzlies. The *ursus horriblus* here pretty much keep to themselves, and are seldom seen.

Imagine our surprise when one came out of the brush pile we'd passed earlier and began trotting up the trail toward us, seeming quite unhappy.

It doesn't pay to make grizzlies unhappy. It's a very bad idea.

I frantically began to try to get the bolt on Jim's rifle to open, and the metal ground with dirt and grit. I put the butt to my shoulder, praying the weapon, now seeming quite underpowered, wouldn't blow up in my face if I had to shoot. And it was looking like I would have to.

The bear reared onto its hind legs, and I began to squeeze the trigger when a coyote's howl echoed through the falling snow. The bear dropped back to all fours, and looked up where the sound had come from, and I eased my finger off the trigger.

A gray doggish shape, difficult to see through the snow, trotted toward the bear, and the two animals looked at each other in the haze, not making a sound. They stood that way for roughly a count of ten, then the bear looked down the trail.

It looked in the direction Cleeve had just run.

And then, the bear took off in the same direction, disappearing into the snow storm.

The doggish shape turned its head toward us, seemed to nod, and then it too, disappeared into the haze of falling snow.

Jim Three Feathers looked at me, eyes kind of wide, and said something in a language I didn't understand. We hobbled on to try and find our people. We were just at the fork in the trail when we heard a scream from down valley. A scream so loud and horrifying that even the falling snow couldn't muffle it.

You couldn't have paid me to go investigate that.

CHAPTER THIRTY-ONE

As so often seems to happen with the cavalry, they were late.

Uncle Gil and Vinnie arrived that evening, and his FBI friends didn't get there until the next midday. They came in the company of some gentlemen from the State Patrol, and shortly thereafter, a heated discussion on jurisdiction ensued.

By their thinking (and the bylaws of Loman County) with the loss of the sheriff, the highest-ranking deputy would take on that duty until the next election. Lincoln Davies took over at that point, becoming the first sheriff of Native American descent that the county had ever known.

Much to my personal surprise, I was deputized by the new sheriff, and tasked with finding the bodies of Bill Farnsworth, the forest service man who'd helped me save Rosa's life when Cleeve's deputies had so treacherously turned on us. During a break in the weather, we borrowed a helicopter and pilot from Okanogan county, and Jim Three Feathers helped find the spot where Bill's body had landed.

The retrieval wasn't very nice. A body impacting hard surfaces at the speed his was traveling doesn't always stay in one piece, and it took three different trips from helicopter to impact point to get him all aboard, in three different bags. The day after that, we retrieved Sheriff Belshaw and all our gear. We also managed to find Holmes, who had left a much more intact corpse than Farnsworth, but one still quite as dead.

We were never able to find Teeg Mason. The wilderness had him, and it wanted to keep him.

I was beat when we drove back from retrieving Farnsworth.
I walked into the station in my ill-fitting uniform, only to find the
girl of my dreams attired the same way.

"You the new sheriff in town, ma'am?" I asked.

"The new dep'ty, mister." She limped over to me and gave me
a kiss that made everything worthwhile.

"That's enough sexual harassment on the job," Uncle Gil said,
walking out of a side office. "Davies and Halloran just called in.
They found Cleeve."

"He didn't make it to Canada, then?" Jim Three Feathers,
following me in the door, looked just as tired as I felt.

"I think we all know he didn't," Uncle Gil said. "They found
him in the valley where you and he had your confrontation. Took
them half a day to find his body."

"So, definitely dead," I said.

"It took them another hour to find what was left of his head,
so... yeah. Dead."

"Yeesh," Rosa said. "Not that he deserved better, but...
yeesh!"

"Maybe now, we can all get our pay and get home," I said.

That was not to be.

The new sheriff, arriving later, said, "Actually, I'm hoping
you all will stay 'til I can get some feelers out there and find new
people to fill the four empty positions we now have." He handed
us photocopied booklets. They were training manuals for sheriff
department new hires.

"Let me make a few calls," Uncle Gil said with a sigh.
"Vinnie's gonna have to hold down the fort until we can get back
home. I'll see if Mac's mom can bring some things up here for us."

"This is only temporary, right?" I said.

"A month, tops," Lincoln said, smiling.

****

Three months later, I was hiking down the steep road, over a
semi-frozen layer of snow, to my small trailer on the shores of the
Columbia River. Rosa was with me.

I was carrying a huge Army Surplus backpack recently purchased
and filled with the possessions I'd been living with for our time up

north, as well as some groceries. I also had my gear I'd originally taken. Rosa was carrying a small overnight bag. My truck was left at the gate, as wintertime was not really a good season to brave the road down to my place.

"Oh man," I said, looking on the little plot of land that contained almost everything I owned. "It was starting to feel like I'd never get back here."

"This place is definitely you," Rosa said, steam from her breath curling out over the drop off. "Did your mom turn on the heat? I hope?"

"She said she did." My mom had been good enough to clean out fridges and turn thermostats down while we were gone, which was good, because I'm not sure I'd ever been busier than the time spent as a temporary Loman County Sheriff Deputy.

After a week of on the job training, sheriff Davies and all of his new deputies went on a meth-seeking rampage throughout the county, much to the joy of many long-term residents. Lincoln and the Loman County prosecutor offered Herman full immunity and a one-way ticket to anywhere he wanted if he would rat out all the other members of Cleeve's little drug kingdom. Herman may have looked like he had the intellect of a lobotomized rat, but he knew the best deal he was going to get when he saw it. By the time we were done, the limited jail space in the county was being used to capacity.

It had taken three months for Davies to fill two of the four empty positions, and to have a list of interviewees to bring to the remote county. However, Uncle Gil had finally rescued all of us by tendering our resignation en masse, citing that his business was suffering greatly from our absence, and we were finally able to come home.

"You heard they found our two 'FBI' guys?" Rosa asked.

"Yeah, two dead guys found at a public fishing parking lot. But no van."

"Should have known car thieves would take it. Bottom line is, no one knows who the men were, what they were doing out there or who shot them. Or why they had fake FBI identification." Rosa said.

"I guess then, that the three S's are still in effect." I told her.

"Except the shoveling, unless you count the snow. I'm sure not planning on saying anything."

"And I doubt Jim, Mike, or Ronnie will either. Doesn't really matter if those men are linked with Cleeve at this point. I think he's paid for his crimes."

We made our way to the trailer and climbed the snow-covered steps. There was a lot less of the white stuff than we had seen up north, but it still covered the deck. I was glad to see that Mom had shoveled out around the door so we could open it.

"She may have turned the heat on," Rosa said, "but she obviously didn't turn it up too far."

"At least it's not freezing," I said, turning the thermostat up to a more humane level.

I went to my sink, and with hope in my heart, turned it on. A trickle of water, about half normal flow dribbled out.

"Great, pipes are not happy," I said, leaving it running.

We unloaded the groceries and left everything else in the overlarge pack, including my old ALICE pack and suspender belt. Looking outside, I saw that the sun had finally cleared the cliffs that lined my "backyard." I made coffee, and pulled two folding lawn chairs out of the shed. Setting them on the deck, we basked in the now quickly warming day in our down coats and winter caps, drinking our coffee.

"The snow will be gone soon, at this rate," I said.

Rosa looked out over the river to the sagebrushed shore on the other side. "I love this place. You're lucky to have found it and worked a deal to buy it."

"As rough as they were, the last three months have given me a little cushion, even let me pay a little bit ahead. You know, Rosa," I said, choking a little trying to get the words out, "you could live down here all the time."

She looked at me with an expression of appraisal. "Are you saying what I think you are, Mac?"

"I… uh… well. You could live here with me. We could see where that leads, that's what I'm saying."

She smiled. "I don't think I'm ready for that, just yet."

"Ah," I said, trying to keep my voice from betraying me.

"Maybe someday." She leaned so close that her lips touched my cheek. "And I did bring my overnight bag."

"Why, yes, I couldn't help but notice that."

"It's been a long and tiring time," She purred, kissing my cheek, "I'm feeling like I might need a... nap... now. Would you like to take a *nap* with me?"

"I'd like to take a nap with you more than anything else I could possibly imagine." Trying not to spring from my chair, I stood. Then I remembered I needed to turn on the pilot light for the water heater before I came in, or the pipes might truly freeze. "Can you give me just a moment to get the water heater going? We'll be sorry if I don't."

"No problem, but don't be long. I'm really... sleepy." She went inside, and I reached in and retrieved the long-nosed lighter I used to turn on the pilot light. I moved around to the back of the trailer at just under the speed of sound, and fumbled with the lighter for a few moments, cursing the inefficiency of technology. It finally lit.

Moving around to the front step, I was stopped in place by what I saw. Fresh coyote tracks, familiar ones that hadn't been there a few minutes before in the semi-hard snow. I looked up the river where they went out of sight, and saw nothing. I shivered for a moment, then shrugged.

I went inside for 'nap time' with my Rosa. Everything else could wait 'til later.

END

Acknowledgments and afterword

Just a note from Clint…
If you haven't figured it out, don't bother looking for Loman County on the map, or the town of McClellan in Loman County. I'm not crazy enough to make the hardworking people of law enforcement bad guys in any county that actually exists. I hold our county sheriffs in the highest regard.

I hope you enjoyed the story, thank you very much for reading it! If you liked it, also note that this is the second of Mac's adventures. The first book in this series is The Sage Wind Blows Cold.

∗∗∗∗∗∗∗∗∗∗∗∗∗∗∗∗∗∗∗∗∗∗∗∗∗∗∗∗∗

Special thanks to Suzette Hollingsworth,
Michele Carter, Editor and
Tina Winograd, Editor

Also by Clint Hollingsworth

The Sage Wind Blows Cold: Mac Crow #1

The Road Sharks: Ghost Wind Chronicles #1

Wandering Ones: Scout Trail (Graphic Novel)

See more or follow me on my Amazon Page!

Or at ClintHollingsworth.com

I hope you enjoyed this new adult thriller which draws on my survival/nature training with Tom Brown, Jr., Earthwork Northwest and Jon Young and my black belt karate training in Goju-ryu. There's much more to come in this Mac Crow series! I have a whole world of adventure for Mac and Rosa.

If you'd like to learn more about my books and graphic novels, you can find more about me at my website, clinthollingsworth.com. If you'd like to keep up with what I am doing, please sign up for my newsletter. It will have book and comic news, articles on survival and nature, general fun musings and links to cool stuff. You can sign up here.

If you enjoyed *Death In The High Lonesome*, it is most appreciated if you could take the time to post a review. These days, authors seem to live or die by the number of reviews they have. It could mean the difference between going back to my day job or continuing my writing career, so I thank you in advance.

My wife, Suzette Hollingsworth, has written a Sherlock Holmes series, if you are in the market for witty banter, mystery, and romance.

If you'd like to read a post-apocalyptic adventure check out *The Wandering Ones* webcomic. If humor is more your game, try our semi-auto biographical webcomic Starting From Scratch.

Thanks for reading!

-Clint Hollingsworth

Mac Crow Thriller #1

The Sage Wind Blows Cold

CLINT HOLLINGSWORTH